MYTHOLOGY BOOK FOR TEENS
LEGENDARY GODS AND HEROES

TABLE OF CONTENTS

INTRODUCTION 6

CHAPTER 1: GREEK MYTHOLOGY 11

    WHAT IS A GREEK MYTH? 11

CHAPTER 2: WHAT IS THE DEFINITION OF MYTHOLOGY?...... 19

CHAPTER 3: WHEN DID GREEK MYTHOLOGY START?............ 29

CHAPTER 4: CONCEPT OF HEROES AND GODS 36

CHAPTER 5: OLYMPIAN GODS.. 44

CHAPTER 6: TWELVE MAJOR DEITIES 49

CHAPTER 7: ZEUS.. 53

CHAPTER 8: ATHENA 60

CHAPTER 9: POSEIDON 63

CHAPTER 10: HERA 68

CHAPTER 11: ARTEMIS.. 71

CHAPTER 12: ACHILLES 78

CHAPTER 13: ACTEON... 86

CHAPTER 14: CALYPSO.. 91

MYTHOLOGY BOOKS FOR TEENS: LEGENDARY GODS AND HEROES

CHAPTER 15: HOMER 94

CHAPTER 16: ODYSSEUS 97

CHAPTER 17: TIRESIAS 101

CHAPTER 18: OEDIPUS 104

CHAPTER 19: HERACLES 110

CHAPTER 20: MEDUSA 115

CHAPTER 21: PROMETHEUS 118

CHAPTER 22: MINOS 121

CHAPTER 23: ORPHEUS 125

CHAPTER 24: DAEDALUS 128

CHAPTER 25: PERSEPHONE AND HADES 133

CHAPTER 26: ORPHEUS' SIBYL AND BACCHUS 136

CHAPTER 27: MYTHOLOGICAL CREATURES 139

CHAPTER 28: VIKINGS OR NORSE MYTHOLOGY 146

 WHAT IS A NORDIC MYTH? 146
 WHY WERE THE VIKINGS IMPORTANT? 146
 WHAT IS THE CONCEPT OF A VIKING GOD AND GODDESS? 149
 WHEN DID THE VIKING MYTH START? 150

CHAPTER 29: AESIR GODS AND ASYNJUR GODDESSES 152

CHAPTER 30: THOR: THE GOD OF THUNDER 155

The Story behind Thor's Hammer 155

Thor's Journey to Asgard 158

Sif 165

Sif's Golden Hair 166

The Giants 171

Ymir 172

Idunn and the Apples of Youth 174

Hermóðr 177

CHAPTER 31: BALDR'S DEATH IN THE TWILIGHT OF THE GODS 183

CHAPTER 32: LOKI'S BLOOD OATH 192

The Bifrost Bridge and the World Tree of Yggdrasil in the Underworld 193

Ragnarok or Twilight of the Gods 195

Yggdrasil and the Nine Worlds 197

CHAPTER 33: EGYPTIAN MYTHOLOGY 201

What Is an Egyptian Myth? 201

Concept of Afterlife 202

What Is the Concept of an Egyptian God or Goddess? 204

CHAPTER 34: HOW WAS ANCIENT EGYPT RULED? 208

CHAPTER 35: RA'S JOURNEY TO THE UNDERWORLD 217

CHAPTER 36: THE BOOK OF THE DEAD AND THE PATH OF OSIRIS 222

CHAPTER 37: THE LIST OF BLACK LANDS AND GATES IN THE UNDERWORLD 228

CHAPTER 38: SETO MAMIUT: GOD OF CHAOS, MAGIC, AND ANIMALS... 236

CHAPTER 39: AMSET, HAPY, DUAMUTEF, QEBEHSENUEF, AND KEBEBASUF IN THE UNDERWORLD 242

CHAPTER 40: HORUS'S JOURNEY TO THE UNDERWORLD..... 248

Nut's Descent into the Underworld...................................... 249

CHAPTER 41: THE END AND THE BEGINNING........................ 253

CONCLUSION.. 257

Introduction

The ancient Greeks told a variety of stories about the gods they worshiped and how these deities interacted with humans. These tales are sometimes amusing, engrossing, and dark, but most importantly, these myths have passed down some of the more useful lessons for living that we still hold today. This book will discuss some of the most important myths and takes an in-depth look at their lessons. It shows us how these stories are relevant to our own lives and how they can help guide our actions. These tales add richness to our lives, as well as a sense of wonder.

The ancient Greeks told many stories about their gods, but there are some that stand out from the rest. These tales have survived to this day and have been retold countless times since first being told. Many of them involve the behavior of humans and how we interact with the gods (and vice versa).

Myths are also important because they help preserve ancient knowledge, traditions, and customs in a format that is fun to read. They can be both entertaining and serious.

Myths are a learning tool for the Greeks, who believe that they should be a way of life rather than just a source of entertainment. They help in understanding our past and who we are. It shows us how to live our lives based on what has worked in the past.

Myths are also important because they can make us reflect on how we live and act today. They teach us lessons about ourselves and the world that can still be applied to modern times.

Mythology books are always a surefire way to feed your intellectual needs. Whether you want to brush up on mythology or have never read one before, this list has something for everyone. From Greek gods and heroes to Norse mythology and Egyptian mythology, these books are perfect for anyone who wants to learn more about mythology without having to dig through dusty old books in some library basement.

If you're looking to delve into mythology, this is the book for you. Featuring over three of the most popular myths worldwide and told from a different angle than most other books, this book will be a surefire hit with any myth lovers. This book is broken down into different cultures with myths, and it tells stories in an enjoyable way. This book would be great if you want to hold onto one book about mythology to give you all of the information in one place.

This book is for anyone who loves mythology or is just curious to learn more about it. This book will tell you about the ideals, customs, and experiences of over three different mythologies. The myths are broken down into parts by culture, and each team will have details on the culture, its significance in the world today, and how mythology may have been influential in the past. This book gives excellent examples of how real people find meaning in myth and their own lives.

If you are fascinated by reading about the types of gods that myths are formed from, this book is for you. It looks at all of the different kinds of gods that people have created to make sense of this world, ranging from animals to plants, planets, and other things people have seen as gods throughout history.

This book is excellent if you want to learn about all of the different myths and legends surrounding ancient Greece. From well-known stories to strange tales that would be new even to most avid myth readers, this book will make you think about all things mythological in an entirely new way.

This book is excellent for anyone who wants to learn more about Egyptian mythology in particular. The book covers the essential legends of ancient Egypt and includes information on various topics, including the gods, religion, magic, and history. Included in this book are facts about Egypt's belief in life after death and the popular gods that were worshippers in Egypt.

Discover the brilliance and wonder that is the Norse people. Go beyond the Marvel comics and pop culture with these unaltered stories. Find out how Thor's hammer helped and destroyed. Discover why Odin's sacrifices are an integral part of the lives of the Norse people before and now. Through mythology, you can journey into the minds of ancient Norse people and find out why we can still learn from history.

The book covers the origins of Greek, Norse, and Egyptian mythologies, the gods and goddesses themselves, and a whole lot of interesting anecdotes and information.

It also has some pictures in it that are great if you want to see what you're reading. The images may not always be excellent, but they get the point across.

Besides its educational value, this book is also fun to read. It tells a story full of remarkable events with heroes and gods who were larger than life. If you haven't read it yet, this old book can be an enjoyable read. You will learn much from it while still being entertained by your choice in literature during your free time.

Chapter 1: Greek Mythology

What Is a Greek Myth?

As you know, the Greeks were a very influential society, and their belief in myths helped form. But what is a Greek myth? Well, a myth is any classic story that explains why things exist. Sometimes it gives meaning to certain rituals. If we take this as accurate, then there are many different ways to tell a myth, such as historical, fantastic, legendary, or dramatic. Within these types, there are two main categories: classical and non-classical myths.

The classical myths have specific cultural values that are important and are passed on from generation to generation. These myths include the Trojan War, Hercules, Romulus and Remus, and Dionysus (Greek god). The non-classical myths do not have any cultural value or meaning to them, and they are not passed down through time. Examples of non-classical Greek myths include Orpheus, Persephone, Apollonius of Tyana, and Perseus in Andromeda.

Myth is a significant historical event because it formed society's beliefs within certain aspects of life, such as family structure or religion. One of the most influential societies, if not the most significant of all time, was the

Greeks. Their myths are fundamental in understanding how they viewed life, how they viewed death, and how they viewed love.

The Greek myths are not a mere guide to what we should believe; they are full of symbolism and meaning that give us clues of the past. They explain how love and death are viewed within society. The Greeks believed in life after death; a person's deceased loved ones were with them for all time. Ghosts were also powerful beings who had power over the living. They did not have enough knowledge to explain how the world worked, but they had plenty of information to know about gods and spirits, which could only be explained through myth.

Greek mythology is vast as it covers many different types of stories, from gods and goddesses to pirates and mythical creatures. In ancient Greek mythology, death was an event that took place after a person died. Some of the gods were friendly, and some were ruthless, but they always represented good and evil. The Greeks also had stories about Crete, which is today called modern-day Greece. It is thought that the god Zeus and his children (the Olympians) fought against the Titans and won. It is said that Crete was filled with beautiful mountain ranges like the Cyclops and many other different things such as Poseidon's trident or Artemis' bow. Greek mythology is the origin of many different stories, and some of them have direct significance to the present day.

For example, Prometheus is a pretty controversial figure because he is credited with causing all the pain humans have suffered due to overpopulation. It would be good to know about his story to understand why we suffer from these problems. The Greeks also learned about the gods of Olympus. Zeus was king of all Olympian gods and had eight other children who were beautiful and lustrous gods: Apollo, Artemis, Athena, Hermes, Aphrodite, Ares, Hephaestus, and Hestia (who was the goddess who protected domestic hearth). The most common type of Greek myth is that of the gods and goddesses. In ancient Greece, they saw the gods as the creators of their lives, and not just Zeus, but other gods like Apollo and Athena were significant. They were known to be mighty entities, and many stories are told about them in their mythology.

In their history, they also thought about what happened after death. The Greeks were blessed with many resources that allowed them to think deeply about life after death. The Greeks saw death as recreation for their past life (the underworld). The central figure in Greek mythology is Hades, who was king of the underworld and had two brothers, Zeus (king of the heavens) and Poseidon (king of the seas). They were constantly arguing with each other, but in the end, they all agreed to have Zeus as the ruler of Olympus (heaven) and Poseidon as his son. Olympus was where all the gods lived and ruled. The Greek gods had home cities, and most were located on Mount Olympus, surrounded by beautiful palaces and lush gardens. The gods made their homes on Mount Olympus while everyone else lived on Earth with nature, other humans, and animals.

One exciting thing that happened is when Zeus had a son named Ares; he was the god of war! Many myths are told about Ares' death: In one instance, he is trying to protect his mother from Hera's jealous attitude toward her husband. Zeus tries to stop the fight, but Hera is more powerful and kills Ares. Another time, Ares killed his brother in a battle over a woman. Zeus was very upset with this situation and asked the Greeks to honor their dead with funeral rites. It shows that they believed in life after death because they knew they would need to bury their dead.

In ancient Greece, death was something that could happen at any time. It was expected for people to die eventually; everyone had an expiration date written into their birth certificate. It's not such a big surprise then when Greek mythology focuses on the subject of death. "The Greeks were fascinated by the subject of death," said mythologist Professor Michael Hetrick. "They believed in life after death, ghosts, and gods who could walk through walls. It was a very mysterious and profound part of their life."

When someone died in ancient Greece, they were thought to go to the underworld, also known as Hades. In the underworld, all the spirits of people who had died came together. These spirits were known as ghosts (or shades) who wandered around and talked with one another for eternity. The underworld was filled with many places and was surrounded by a river Styx. This river had a powerful current that was impossible to swim against; it was said that only a person's soul could cross it into the underworld. However, some people could get across: mostly heroes and men of power because they were blessed with strength far above other people.

According to Greek mythology, the underworld is divided into Hades, Persephone, and Tartarus. The underworld was where all the dead went after they died. The underworld is a place of suffering and sadness throughout history. It's a place of deep darkness filled with weeping and wailing; it's where the souls of the dead would live or rest until they were called for by their gods or other souls who wanted their presence in life.

The Greeks, though, believed that there are two kinds of death: one is "physical" death (meaning death due to sickness), and the other is "spiritual" death (meaning when your soul leaves your body). This "spiritual" death is when a soul departs its body and goes to the underworld. It is what happens if you die due to sickness or other factors such as being killed.

In the underworld, each person's spirit would be judged by the judges who lived there. Some things happened inside the underworld that is just as important to know about: Tartarus was where disobedient heroes were punished. It also had a dark forest with monsters and other monsters that the gods created to punish the Titans. Tartarus also has a pool of water that is called the Lake of Styx, which is known as being the most contaminated water in all creation; it is said that if you put your foot into this lake, then your soul cannot leave. This lake forms the border between Hades and Tartarus; it separates all the places into separate parts.

Inside of Hades, there is a place called the Fields of Asphodel. It is located in the underworld's lower regions, where the dead go who died by violence. It is a place known for its beauty; people who have been long dead would visit this place and enjoy the flowers that bloom there. The flowers draw the eyes with their beauty and happiness.

The River Styx is known as a place where people who commit murder and other major crimes go; it is said to be filled with large snakes, at least the males of them, while the females are harmless.

Those who are innocent and have worshiped the gods go to a place called the Elysian Fields. This is a place where Zeus sends heroes.

The last main place is Tartarus, one of the most important places in the underworld. Tartarus is known as being where the Titans went, for they were punished for their crimes against the Olympians. Many creatures of Hades are also kept in Tartarus. Some of the most significant creatures are Typhon (the giant serpent) and Cerberus (the three-headed dog).

In Hades, there is a place that is filled with all kinds of fruit. This place is known as Elysium, where heroes and others who worship the gods go after they die. The major part of Elysium is filled with different flowers and plants that bloom in this place.

Another place in the underworld is known as the Asphodel Fields. This place is filled with flowers that grow tall and also has some areas that are mostly clouds. It is where heroes who were killed or died by accident go after they died. There is also a place that is filled with poppies and ambergris, which are used to make perfumes and flavors for food. According to Greek myth, this field is a beautiful place where souls gather at a feast. Actually, this place is said to be very heavenly; it is the closest to heaven that mortals can get. People who belong in the Asphodel Fields, though, can't go through the river Styx and get out of the underworld.

Chapter 2: What Is the Definition of Mythology?

Mythology is "a body of oral tradition concerning gods, heroes, and other supernatural beings who can be said to be part of a culture's collective memory." Hence, the word *mythology* means "stories about mythological beings."

The term is also used in the study of literature. In this sense, mythology denotes offhand narrative details included in many poems and stories. It may consist of prominent events even though they are not an essential part of the story and scenes that need not have happened.

The word *mythology* is often used as a synonym for *myth*, which is technically incorrect. The term *mythology* refers to the study of myths in general, while myths are stories that include supernatural beings and happenings. In this sense, any report that provides for fantastic elements can be termed a myth.

Thus, the two terms are not synonymous, and neither is a subset of the other. For example, the story of Karna in Mahabharata cannot be termed mythology because it does not involve supernatural beings. Still, King Arthur's tales in Arthurian myths do contain bizarre characters and may be considered mythology.

It is also essential to understand that mythologies belong to specific regions. For example, there are different mythologies in Japan and India. So using the term "Greek mythology" to mean "Greek mythology and Japanese mythology" is incorrect since the term refers to a separate collection of stories in Greece and Japan.

Mythologies do not exist solely in the oral form either and were written down by the poet Homer around 800 BCE. They were passed on as popular stories until they were eventually written down as Greek mythology and other mythologies. Other legends like Japanese myths surfaced later, but they also include reports from existing oral traditions passed on for generations.

Since all cultures have their mythologies, one may wonder why even Greek myths exist today. After all, the ancient Greeks had no written script, and they lived far away from other cultures in which these myths still exist. One answer is that many people have preserved stories from oral traditions through oral transmission over thousands of years. Another reason for Greek myths surviving is that authors write them down during specific historical periods.

Similar to other mythologies, Greek myths developed over a long period. Many people and events were absorbed into the tales as they were passed on from generation to generation. The ancient Greeks included deities borrowed from their neighbors, and they were eventually integrated into the existing legends. Interestingly, several versions of Greek myths exist in modern times. For example, the story of Heracles has many versions, including the ones by Homer and Hesiod and that by the Roman poet Ovid.

As mythological stories are passed down through time, they may change or acquire new elements to reflect changes in society. By studying these changes, one can gain knowledge about a culture's past. For example, ancient Greek myths contain many references to a theme known as beauty and how it can be acquired. After all, these are universal messages that appeal to people of all ages. Other myths like the story of Oedipus illustrate how a person's social status may change over time. That is why many contemporary stories have changed their purpose. For example, the levels of Homer were once based on an earlier myth of Perseus, but now it has become a tale about love. Indeed, many stories like this contain many themes such as love, justice, and morality.

Background: Greek mythology is the vast body of myths and religions widely known in Greek culture. It was formed almost 4,000 years ago by adding and retelling stories about the gods, heroes, monsters, and other legendary figures worshiped before or after they lived. These stories were often related by ancient Greek poets and playwrights and passed down through oral traditions for thousands of years. In other cultures such as Egypt and Mesopotamia (ancient Iraq), similar stories are also known as folklore.

Despite its popularity, mythology is less understood than most other categories of literature because it touches on subjects like creation, religion, morals, practices, and beliefs. The story of the origin of the world according to Greek myth can be found in Hesiod. Some scholars believe that these stories were popular because they helped give ancient people an understanding of life and the universe.

Greek myths have had a strong influence on almost all forms of literature ever since they were first written down in about 800 BC by Homer. These stories remain popular today and are regularly retold in books, films, and stage plays.

What is the difference between mythology and religion?

The main difference between Greek mythology and other mythologies around the world is that Greek mythology contains supernatural beings that ancient Greeks worshiped. It distinguishes it from other mythologies in which these beings did not have worshipers, and they are referred to as gods or spirits. The main gods of Greek mythology include Zeus, Hercules, Hera, Artemis, Athena, Apollo, and Poseidon.

The stories about these gods are known as myths but are also called legends. They contain accounts of how each god was worshiped, their character traits, and how they helped people differently. Some myths also include stories of heroic deeds performed by the gods.

What subjects are included in Greek myths?

Many of the most famous Greek myths include themes such as love, justice, morals, and beauty. They also have stories that may seem bizarre and silly to us who live in modern times. However, many people today still admire these stories and even discuss them with others. One example is the story of Theseus, whose wife, Ariadne, fell in love with him while he was on a dangerous quest for the Golden Fleece. When she realized that he would marry another woman, she drew a sword and thanked her fate for dying by his side. After she died, he married

Metis, the daughter of Minos, king of Crete. In the end, though, Theseus and Ariadne's love was renewed, and they were reunited in the underworld.

How are Greek myths different from other stories?

The difference between Greek myths and other stories is that they are more ancient than many others, so they often contain more information about people who lived thousands of years ago. For example, these stories can tell us which gods were worshiped or how people lived during this period. However, some stories like *Oedipus Rex* do not seem to have much interest in ancient Greece despite their age. It is because these stories are still popular today.

Greek mythology is sometimes referred to as mythology. Again, it is the study of myths. Instead of being confined to the written word, the stories can also be relived in paintings, pantomimes, or stages. Many people who understand the Greek myths may also talk about them daily or describe something they have experienced themselves.

Do all the Greek myths work at school?

It was initially believed that only some of the Greek myths were required at school; however, research has recently shown that all of them should be studied by students. The first part is about the essential meaning. Students will understand that some gods wanted to become humans to marry people and have children. Famous stories include the story of Jason, *Oedipus Rex*, and Hercules.

The next part is called "analyzing." Analysis means that students will see how some ancient myths have similarities in different cultures. They will also look at different symbols or myths used in different cultures, such as Easter Island (São Paulo) and Easter Island (Tahiti).

Who should study the Greek myths?

All the students in primary education should study Greek myths as part of their curriculum. However, they should follow a specific path through their lessons to use all of them effectively. After seeing the Greek myths, students should understand how people have used different legends to express themselves in different cultures.

The Greek myths are divided into two parts. The first part is called classical mythology, and it goes back to the third century. The second part is called Hellenistic mythology, and it was written in the second century. Although the two parts have some similarities, they do differ in many important aspects, so each part should be studied separately rather than mixing them together, as it would be confusing and difficult to understand them as a whole (Walsh, 1983).

The Greek myths have some similarities to the stories of other cultures. For example, the story of the fall of a world in myth is common to all cultures. The most famous legend is that of Baucis and Philemon, in which a couple is saved from death by a goddess who allows them to go on living forever (Bryant & Bryant, 1999). However, another fact that needs to be taken into consideration is that these myths were made up by different people at different times (Walsh, 1983). This means that the myths now are not an exact picture of a traditional story.

Why teach Greek myths to teens?

Teenagers, especially during the years of adolescence, are interested in the supernatural world. They also want to know their future lives because of their curiosity and natural desire to grow. In other words, they are likely to have an interest in Greek myths. It will be easier for them to understand these myths if they learn them in class. They will also learn the important messages these myths carry. These messages can be a guide for teenagers in their future lives.

What is the best way to teach Greek myths to teens?

Students need to learn not only Greek myths but also the overview of Latin and Norse mythologies. These three mythologies have similarities. Students can compare these mythologies and study the most significant parts of each one. This approach is known as comparative mythology. In addition, teens will be more interested in these myths if they are applicable to their daily lives. They can study the myths and discuss the practical ways to use them in their lives.

What makes Greek myths different from other kinds of myths?

All kinds of myths have a common origin due to the basic human nature and natural desires of human beings. However, Greek myths are familiar to most people because they have been used in several modern stories, such as those in *Lord of the Rings* by J. R. R. Tolkien. In many movies, such as *Clash of the Titans* and *300*, Greek myths have been used as subjects. In contrast to Norse myths, Greek myths appear more historical and more structured. In other words, they are more logical for students to study because they are relatable to teenagers' lives.

What are the benefits of Greek myths for teens?

Greek mythology is an interesting subject to study, and it can be beneficial for a teenager's future. Myths contain values on life that have remained unchanged in the history of Western civilization. They also present different approaches to values. The lessons they learn in these myths can be a guide for teenagers in their lives. In addition, some myths can be used as a reference in today's movies, adding to students' interest.

Chapter 3: When Did Greek Mythology Start?

Greek mythology is a very ancient and rich tradition of stories that began to be told about three thousand years ago. These have been carried down from generation to generation, and there are already different versions of the myths. These stories were created as a way for people to explain the world.

Many gods and goddesses are mentioned in Greek mythology, such as Zeus, Apollo, and Athena. One group of these gods were known as Titans. They preceded the Olympian gods (the Titans' descendants). Other groups include nymphs (spirits) and heroes (men who had done something great).

Greek mythology began with the ancient Greeks. They were advanced people who had schools, theaters, gymnasiums, and art. They had developed an alphabet (the letters of which were a set of lines, making it easier to write on the clay tablets used before). Many great thinkers emerged from that time, including Socrates, Plato, and Aristotle. However, these people also created different gods. They had very human-like qualities, such as having flaws and being jealous or vengeful.

In Greek mythology, there is Pandora's box. It is about a woman whose husband gives her a box but tells her not to open it. However, she opens it, and all of humanity's evil, including death and pain, comes out of it. This myth is thought to be a metaphor for hope.

Greek mythology is still well known today because of its exciting stories and characters. It is also the basis of many works of art. Some examples are TV shows, plays, films, and video games that have been based on myths from thousands of years ago.

Greek mythology has been changing and adapting. For example, the story of Helen of Troy was from the Trojan War myth. Helen, a princess of Sparta, was taken as a prisoner to Troy by Paris of Troy. The idea came about because Homer wrote about this in his poem about the war.

The names given to different characters in Greek mythology have changed over time. They change depending on which region they are from. For example, some gods and goddesses were known by many different names. The most common term used for Zeus is Jupiter (although he may also be called Saturn).

Some people believe that if you know about Greek mythology, it will help you to understand other languages. It is because the Greek language has influenced all other languages we speak today. Also, the structure of words and grammar in the English language comes from Greek and Latin words.

Many vital philosophers came from Greece, including Socrates and Aristotle, and myths are an essential part of everyday life for many Greeks.

The Greeks believe that Zeus was the creator of all the gods and humans, and they celebrate the start of each year on his birthday, which is August 14. In addition to critical religious festivals within Greece, the Greeks celebrate their mythology by dressing up in costumes and having processions.

Nowadays, myths are loved by many people worldwide as they can relate to them personally. For example, some people believe that obeying your parents or teachers is like following Zeus when he was in control.

Greek mythology is part of Greek culture and customs. One example of this is a tradition called the Megaride. The Megaride is the custom of wearing white garments, usually to celebrate spring. It was believed to be like when Zeus took the form of an eagle and made clouds white to start spring. People also wear white clothes during other important dates, such as Easter and

Christmas, for similar reasons. It is also believed that Zeus gave man the natural ability to see in the dark using their eyes so that they could find their way home after leaving their summer homes without getting lost or being caught by predators.

Because the ancient Greeks created Greek mythology, it has many similarities with other cultures. However, it is very different from most other mythologies because of its humor and more human-like qualities.

The myths are spread worldwide because they were written down in books by many different writers and artists in many different languages over a long time. As a result, these myths have been translated into many languages to help explain them to people worldwide. Other writers and artists have created a different interpretation of these myths to fit their own culture, which will sometimes differ from another writer/artist's understanding of the same myth. The Bible is an excellent example of how religion can change depending on where it is being interpreted.

Some people have argued that myths are not entirely accurate. For example, some claim that the Minotaur story was based on actual events and not a tale by a Greek writer.

The city-state of Sparta was supported by many warriors during their time. They have many significant mythological figures, such as King Leonidas. Sparta stayed neutral in wars and made substantial contributions to philosophy and culture, allowing the Spartans to be one of the potent forces in ancient Greece.

Among these people were famous artists, such as Phidias, who sculpted several statues of gods for the Parthenon in Athens. His most famous sculpture is the massive statue of Athena (now called the lost masterpiece of Phidias). Some other celebrated Greek artists include Polygnotus, who painted the frescoes in the Thalamegos Painter's House in Athens.

Greek mythology has been used in many works outside of its own culture, including many literature and visual arts works. The myths will continue to be loved and appreciated by new generations for years to come.

Greek mythology plays a significant role in Western culture. One example is how Greek mythological characters appear in movies or books. Greek mythology has also influenced many Western heroes. Many Western heroes have been portrayed as gods. Hercules and Zeus in Greek mythology are like Batman and Superman in American popular culture. The famous warrior Achilles was inspired by Achilles Tatius, a hero from the Trojan War.

Another example of how Greek mythology has affected Western culture is its role in its past. Ancient Greece was more than just a civilized civilization that preserved myths; it was also a collection of many different cultures and societies at once that all contributed to a standard set of values and beliefs. One example of this is the rise of Western philosophy. The writings of Plato, Pythagoras, and Aristotle are some of the most influential philosophical writings in Western civilization. Another example is the tragedy genre in Western literature, which is inspired by Aeschylus, Sophocles, and Euripides.

Greek mythology made a significant impact on other Western cultures as well. For example, Greek mythology is believed to have influenced the Jewish culture in many aspects, such as the story of Hercules, which was later adopted in the Book of Judges. It is just one example of how Greek mythology has impacted all areas of Western culture.

Mythology is also present in popular literature even today. Modern retellings of ancient myths are still very popular and are constantly being created; notable examples include *The Lightning Thief* and *Percy Jackson & the Olympians*.

The Greco-Roman style of architecture has also influenced Western culture. An example is the Parthenon in Athens, a temple dedicated to the goddess Athena and is now a World Heritage site. Other well-known examples include the Colosseum in Rome and the Roman Forum.

Most Western holidays and festivals have their origins in the celebrations held by ancient Greeks and Romans. The most notable examples are Christmas (based on pagan European winter festivals), Easter, Thanksgiving, Halloween (a celebration of the harvest), Valentine's Day (based on Lupercalia), and Carnival (based on Roman festivals). Another example is sports events such as the Olympic Games.

Chapter 4: Concept of Heroes and Gods

Hero refers to a mortal chosen by the gods for an extraordinary fate. It's a word with several meanings in English — it can be the name of someone who is admired, an idealized version of oneself, or even one's conscience. A hero is often thought to possess certain traits, such as:

- Bravery
- Courage
- Intelligence
- Vigilance
- Virtue
- Fortitude (also called resiliency)
- Determination
- Moral conviction
- Strength of character

In Greek mythology, heroes are sometimes called demigods. They share the immortality of their divine parent, but most demigods are human. A hero's journey is usually the story of the duration and trials in a hero's life. Their exploits are required to be great and large to be considered heroes.

There are many different types of heroes. They also come in many characteristics, and there are male heroes, female heroes, child heroes, and even animal heroes. In Greek mythology, heroes were people with the courage to fight for what they believed was right. Most Greek heroes were warriors that fought against monsters or other creatures that threatened both their home city-states and countries, as well as the gods themselves.

In a society that is governed by the male gender, female heroes often go unnoticed or are given less praise. While there are many well-known male heroes in Greek mythology, there are just as many female heroes, but they don't recognize it. In Greek mythology, the most famous of these heroines is Andromache, a wife and queen of the Trojan War hero Hector. Even though she married a prince and queen, we do not know much about her life other than what is mentioned in Homer's *The Iliad*, which we will discuss later.

Heroes are often thought to be smarter than ordinary humans because of their near-divine status and constant dealings with the gods. Through their experience with the gods, they gain a wealth of knowledge and understanding. If a monster is terrorizing a city, the hero will typically not be afraid to face it. Heroes are also courageous or willing to risk death for what they believe.

Heroes are often thought of as possessing many virtues and characteristics that make them who they are. Some of these include courage, endurance, honor, wisdom, and bravery. This list could go on forever because heroes often display different virtues depending on who you ask or which stories you read. Most heroes had some divine ancestry to become immortal in the first place but were also mortal because they were born from a dead mother or man. The only proper way to become immortal was to be a child of the god Zeus. Originally, heroes were born fully mortal and would gain their supernatural abilities once they went through a series of trials or quests. These trials made them heroes first and are one of the most well-known myths in Greek mythology. An example of this is the Argonauts, who went on a quest to get the Golden Fleece from King Aeetes by going through all his challenges and getting past all his dangers. Another example is Jason, who was part of the Argonauts. He had to take back the kingdom of Medea's father from her brother Aietes by going on another quest with Jason's lover Medea.

The gods were the original creators and the most demanding judge of any hero. The gods in Greek mythology were very easily angered. For this reason, most heroes had to perform many tasks for the gods and often quests that would prove to them just how worthy they were of being a hero.

For example, Heracles' twelve labors showed how brave, strong, and capable Heracles was of completing such heavy tasks as killing a Hydra, capturing two Erymanthian boars alive, and cleaning the stable of King Augeias of its manure.

Greek heroes also believed that once their work for the gods was done and the task completed, they must return to being mortal humans. Because of this, most heroes remained in their town or village and often returned to their family home, where they stayed until the day they died. Most Greek heroes lived to be old and had many adventures, and they even became rulers in their cities or countries.

However, there are some examples of Greek heroes who don't fit well into this pattern, such as Hercules, who eventually left his beloved wife, Hebe, behind him on his quest for immortality (by mating with her).

In Greek mythology, heroes were often thought of as people who lived a life of suffering. Most heroes suffered many hardships but were given great respect for completing their adventure or quest. To be a hero, one must go through great struggles and face many obstacles.

The myths usually revolve around the hero protecting his city-state and country from various monsters and evil creatures that threaten them all. The hero is the only one fit for such a task because he or she has been bestowed with supernatural powers by the gods to defeat these evil foes.

While many heroes are the results of divine intervention, many acted as heroes in their own right.

Some heroes went through great trials to be what they are today, and others were born heroes. Many stories revolve around them overcoming many obstacles and monsters that have come at them in the past, attempting to end their quest for glory or immortality. Some even had to fight against their family because they thought they wouldn't survive such inquiries.

Heroes can often have a very epic and heroic phase in their lives. Many heroes will go on quests and face many dangers to complete their search for immortality.

Some heroes result from divine intervention, but sometimes a person is destined from birth to be a hero. These heroes are often born on the day that a god was in human form (or people similar to them). The gods used these special people for everyday tasks they needed to be completed and rewarded them with great power. Other heroes are not born from any divine intervention but from nature (such as Athena being the daughter of Zeus) and even simple interests.

Greek heroes come in all shapes, sizes, and allegiances. Most heroes are famous for their physical strength, bravery, and perseverance. Most Greek heroes also had a love life with many affairs and intrigue behind the scenes from the gods.

However, some Greek heroes were known for overcoming hardship after hardship to succeed in their quest. A select few Greek heroes are known for their great deeds every day and sometimes even today! For example, Achilles is considered by many historians as one of the greatest heroes in history because his legacy lived on long after his death. Although he was a mortal man who suffered enormously throughout his journey and life, his story inspires people.

These Greek heroes are the type of people whom we should look up to today as an example in life. If these Greek heroes can overcome such incredible obstacles and still be successful, then so can we!

We've all heard of these legendary heroes that have numerous stories and tales surrounding them. These are some of the greatest Greek heroes from antiquity.

Because they were so great, their stories continue to be told to this day and even be notified for decades to come. We should never forget the heroic deeds these people did to overcome hardships in life and be successful.

These heroes have many things in common. They all were leaders and warriors. You can find many of these heroes mentioned in the myths where they are quite well known. All of them were considered to be great individuals in their time, and they even had good traits that aided their achievements. In most cases, they didn't always have a good nature and had many flaws, but this just made them even more appealing for us to learn from because we could relate to their struggles and how they overcame adversity. There is one thing that each of these heroes had in common as well. They were all considered heroes, and they all are important to the history of Greece. It was a time when the world was more about self-service and doing what you want instead of thinking about others. That changed as years went on. People started to look at others because their self-interest became more important for survival, especially during the time of war. All of these heroes defied that idea, and they went beyond what others demanded them to do. They were accepted by their community and society because they were feared. No one wanted to mess around with a great hero, so people would listen to them, do what they asked for, and not have fights with them. Many of the great heroes had dark sides. Many people wonder where they came from, but that didn't stop the public from admiring their heroic traits. This is why the great heroes have become a major part of Greek mythology.

Chapter 5: Olympian Gods

How to be an Olympian God? To be immortalized in legend and mythology for all time, you had better have some pretty impressive qualities. So how does one achieve a god-like status? Here are the key traits of those who have become immortalized in mythology:

Strength and Beauty

The Greeks believed that without strength or beauty, you would not achieve immortality. Modern-day people might disagree on what constitutes strength or beauty, but there is no doubt that they were both necessary if you wanted your name written in eternity.

Cunning and Intelligence

To be immortalized in mythology, you had better have a certain level of cunning and intelligence to elevate you above the humans around you. The Greeks believed that a god must be clever enough to want to be a god. The symbol of an owl was often used to signify wisdom and cunning. A certain level of cunning and intelligence is needed to elevate you above the humans around you.

Ingenuity

This trait is one of the most useful when it comes to ascension as it allows you to create an identity for yourself in the world. In Greek mythology, Prometheus made man out of clay, and Athena created man out of gold, so they could both escape from being confined by mere mortal men. To be immortalized in classical mythology, you had better have invented something beneficial and unique to enhance your reputation and desired level of power. Ingenuity is the most useful trait when it comes to ascension as it allows you to make an identity for yourself in the world.

Being a Hero

When someone designs something special or creates some beautiful story, they will naturally become known as heroes to all those around them. They may not necessarily achieve god-like status, but their name will still be remembered for many generations to come.

Those are the main traits of those who achieved immortality and ascension to Olympian godhood in classical mythology. Only a very select few people reached such great heights, but this is mainly due to their unique qualities.

Who are the Olympian gods? An Olympic pantheon is a group of twelve significant deities and sometimes includes the four minor gods. Notably, all of these gods are male. Every time Zeus sits on his father's throne in heaven in Greek mythology, he unknowingly slips a thunderbolt into his left hand while grabbing power with his right hand. This section will list the top things you need to know about Olympian gods!

The first thing to know is that they represent forces in nature like chance (Tyche), time (Horae), or war (Deimos). Another thing to know is that they are the children of either Zeus or Kronos. Third, they exist in several realms, from the Elysian Fields to Tartarus. The most important is Mount Olympus, which is where all the gods stay. However, Hades (god of the underworld) and his realm are another integral part of this pantheon. Also, you can find them in Elysium and Hades' realm Tartarus.

Below is a list of gods and goddesses in order of their importance:

1. Father Zeus: He is the King of the Cosmos and Lord of Olympus.
2. Father Kronos: He overthrew his father after an altercation with his mother, Rhea.

3. Mother Rhea: She is the goddess of Earth and Rancor. She had an affair with her father, Gaea (Gaia).
4. Hephaestus (Hephaestos): He is the Smith, god of fire and the forges for the Olympian gods.
5. Ares: He is the god of war.
6. Aphrodite: She is the goddess of love and beauty and the lover of Hermes and many mortal men.
7. Hermes: He is the messenger of the gods and patron god of thieves.
8. Apollo: He is the god of light and medicine. He also conducted oracles.
9. Demeter: She is the goddess of agriculture and harvest in the Hellenic religion. She is associated with grain and flowering plants and their growth in fields. She presided over crops in which she was honored with human sacrifices. In her honor, many festivals were held, and Greek men would become intoxicated and celebrate the end of the harvest season.
10. Dionysus: He is the god of wine and parties. He is sometimes referred to as "the Liberator" because he frees people from their responsibilities.
11. Aphrodite: She is the goddess of love, lust, and beauty.

12. Hera: She is the queen of the gods, protecting marriage and women's role in society. She is Zeus' sister and is jealous of Zeus' affairs with mortal women.
13. Hephaestus (Hephaestos): He is the god of fire. He makes all the weapons used by gods, such as arrows for Apollo, swords for Ares, or guns for Hermes.
14. Artemis: She is the goddess of the hunt and moon. She is a goddess of virgins who protects women in childbirth. She also cares for the young animals.
15. Hephaestus (Hephaestos). He is the god of fire.
16. Poseidon: He is the god of the sea.
17. Dawn: She is the goddess of the dawn. She is a minor goddess who rules over the morning.
18. Hebe: She is the goddess of youth and fertility. She presides over the marriage ceremony and marriage itself.

Chapter 6: Twelve Major Deities

This chapter will provide you with basic facts about twelve significant deities in Greek mythology. From Zeus (the ruler of Olympus) and Hera (his queen) to Hermes (the god of merchants and thieves), there is a lot to learn about these figures. After reading this chapter, you will have an understanding of the key players in Greek mythology.

Zeus

Also known as the king, Zeus is the supreme god in Greek mythology. He is the ruler of Olympus, and his wife, Hera, rules Mount Olympus. The twelve gods and goddesses all reside on Mount Olympus.

Hera

She is the queen of heaven and a daughter of Cronus (the Greek word *cronos* means "time"). Hera is also mentioned as a daughter of Zeus in some myths and had consorts such as Dione, Eileithyia, and Eris (the goddess who brought discord into the world).

Hermes

He is one of the gods who rule over commerce. He rides through Mount Olympus at regular intervals, bringing news to his father Zeus and his sisters Hera and Aphrodite (the goddess of love). Hermes also acted as a messenger for Zeus' father, Cronus.

Aphrodite

She is a goddess of love. She is the goddess in charge of marriages, and she is the daughter of Zeus. She is also known as Aphrodite Urania (*Urania* means "born from the sea"). Aphrodite is said to have been conducted on the island of Cyprus from an egg laid by a great fish called Thetis or Demeter and her son called Pontus or Cronus.

Apollo

His father is Zeus and the brother of Artemis (the goddess of the moon and hunt). In Greek mythology, he is known for his oratory skill. He is also known as Apollo Delphinios (Delphinios means Apollo's dolphin) because he rides on a dolphin. Delphinios is derived from the word *delphos*, which refers to a dolphin.

Artemis

He is a daughter of Zeus and a sister of Apollo. She also has a twin brother called Apollo. The twin is known as Artemisia or Atropos (meaning the hand that cuts the thread). Artemis is the goddess of the moon. She is also worshipped as a virgin; she does not have children or a husband.

Ares

Ares means "warlike." He is the god of war and is seen as the opposite of his twin brother, Aphrodite. He is also known as Mars, a warrior god in Roman mythology.

Poseidon

He is called the earth-shaker. He is the brother of Hades, who is also known as Pluto and ruler of the underworld. His cult center is at Corinth, and he has many temples across Greece in the cities such as Corinth, Athens, and Delphi. Like Hades, Poseidon is also a god with sharp teeth.

Hephaestus

He is known as the god of fire and metalworking. He has a temple (Thesmophoria) in Athens, and he is said to be the son of Zeus and Hera. Hephaestus was exiled from Olympus at one point in his life, but later, he returned.

Athena

She is the goddess of wisdom and is the daughter of Zeus. She is also known as Minerva, the goddess of weaving.

Demeter

She is the goddess of agriculture and earth. She is the mother of Persephone, who is also known as Kore (meaning "maiden"). Demeter does not have any consorts or children; her closest companion in mythology would be her daughter Protos (meaning "younger child").

Hestia

She is the daughter of Zeus. Hestia is the goddess of hearth and home. She has no consort or children, and she did not marry even, although some myths say that she did get married to Poseidon (the Greek god of earthquakes).

Dionysus or Bacchus

He is the god of wine and fertility who may have been the son of Zeus. Dionysus is also known as Bacchus (meaning "one who has the power to intoxicate"). He is seen as the god responsible for nature, but he is also seen as a subversive force.

Chapter 7: Zeus

Who is Zeus?

Zeus is a major god in Greek mythology. He is the son of Cronus and Rhea and the youngest of his siblings. Zeus has many children with goddesses (known as the Olympians), but some of his well-known extramarital affairs resulted in offspring like Athena. He is known for fighting off Typhon, saving Olympus on more than one occasion, launching a thunderbolt that led to war between the Titans and gods. He wielded an ax, making him responsible for lightning bolts that turned out to be destructive, even though he could end wars with them too. The Romans called Zeus Jupiter.

What was the Olympians' mission?

As the ruler of the gods, Zeus gave them a mission to protect the mortals and make sure they lived in peace. He assigned them to different places and transformed them into new creatures that had supernatural powers. He also made sure their enemies were not able to cause any harm to the mortals.

What is Zeus' personality?

Zeus is a wise and powerful god who loved his creatures. He punished those who did evil things, but he didn't do anything terrible to them unless they harmed others. His most famous decisions were the punishment of his siblings, Poseidon and Hades, when they both tried to overthrow him.

How did Zeus die?

The Greeks said that Zeus died from an illness because it was too hard for him to continue ruling the world. According to this belief, Zeus is now buried on the island of Naxos.

What made Zeus act selfishly?

When Hera, Zeus' wife, learned that Aphrodite and others were loving Adonis and that he was staying in the woods near Mycenae, she became furious because she believed that Adonis would endanger their son's life. She told Athena that Zeus should get rid of Adonis and punish Aphrodite for causing him to be in love with her and cause trouble.

How did Zeus act selfishly?

Zeus then sent one of his eagles to grab Adonis by the hair and carry him off to Olympus, where he was sentenced to live with Aphrodite for eternity. That was not the only thing Zeus had done that made him lose sympathy from his people. For example, when he returned from Pan's wedding and encountered a drunken Athena, he failed to control himself; instead of showing sympathy toward her, he changed her into a white cow in anger. On an occasion when Zeus was looking down from Olympus to earth and saw Hera's son, Ares, making a mess of the world, instead of allowing his wife to take care of their son, Zeus made Ares into a god. He also punished Helen by turning her into Helen of Troy and gave the beautiful King Priam the task of guarding her forever.

How can anyone love Zeus?

If someone loves Zeus or wants to serve him, he is most likely to follow his ideals and beliefs and do good things for others. It could also be that people hope that he will reward them one day. Those who choose to betray Zeus in any way often end up suffering very severely for it. It shows that anyone who loves Zeus with a pure heart will be rewarded for their loyalty. Those who don't love him because they hate what he does should think twice before doing anything that would make Zeus feel badly of them; they could end up living in the underworld for all eternity.

How did the Greeks view Zeus?

Some ancient Greek myths and legends depict Zeus differently from the way we now view him. For example, some stories explain that he was not always the god of thunder, but rather, it was Zeus' rage first brought upon by Hera during their relationship that caused an early thunderstorm to occur. Other stories say that he ruled with wisdom and patience that the people will not worry about anything. Future Greek generations would then use his name to give him a new title—the god of kingship.

Did the Greek Gods exist?

Zeus is a Greek and Roman name. It means "light of the sky" or perhaps something similar to this. He is the god of sky and thunder, often considered equivalent to Jupiter in Roman mythology. He is also associated with fire, law and order; kingship, war, fertility, agriculture, justice, military strategy, weather control, benefactions on human beings and crops (he gave us wheat), and sex.

It is often argued that Zeus or Jupiter was never considered gods in any ancient society. Quite the contrary, most people of antiquity saw themselves as simple humans toiling away in their work-a-day lives. They were minor figures in a hierarchical system of Egyptian deities and other entities that existed only to govern lesser entities and beings. They had no particular role to play.

Zeus, the king of Olympus, had several wives.

In ancient Greek times, Zeus was married to Hera. This marriage was unhappy because Hera was jealous of Zeus' other lovers. To punish him, she made Adonis fall in love with Aphrodite and take her as a lover. Aphrodite also fell in love with Adonis, so she took him as her lover too. It infuriated both Hera and Zeus so much that they decided to get rid of Adonis but first decided to punish Aphrodite and sent an eagle to seize him by his hair and carry him up to Olympus, where he was sentenced to live for eternity with Aphrodite.

Later, Aphrodite found out that Adonis was deceased, and she mourned for him. She made a tree grow out of his blood—the myrtle. His death left such a terrible impact on her; she made a festival in his honor. It is the reason why people celebrate carnivals today.

Zeus married two other goddesses as well: Metis and Maia. The child of Zeus and Maia is Hermes, and the child of Zeus and Metis is Athena. Many other Zeus' wives, including Leto, Alcmene, Daphne, Semele, Io, and Europe. Zeus also fathered creatures such as the horse, the lion, the eagle, and many others.

Zeus is the father of all gods because he is regarded as omnipotent. He has other children like Athena, Hermes, Dionysus, and Apollo. His brothers were Poseidon and Hades, while his sisters were Hestia, Demeter, and Hera. He has more than a thousand children with goddesses but only fifty children with mortal women. The goddesses who gave birth to his children included Demeter, Mnemosyne, Leto, and Hera.

The Titans were the immediate descendants of Zeus. He was the first one to be born to his parents. The Titans are also known as the Cyclopes, Hekatonkheires, and Brontes. They were among the first generation of gods and men. These were fire-breathing giants who lived on Mount Kaukasos near Sinope. They were cloned and had three eyes and six hands full of fingers. Some of them could produce thunder by clapping their hands or projecting some lightning through their fingers, or smacking their thighs loudly with their hands. Some of them were also reputed to possess the power of foretelling future events.

The Titans were later overthrown by Zeus and replaced by the Olympian gods. They ruled the world until the age of man. Zeus had taught his children that they would be punished if they defied him. The Kritias, who told them how to build a chariot to escape from their dungeon, is one example of this punishment. He had saved Prometheus, who was chained to a rock in the Caucasus Mountains by giving him a poisonous snake on his liver every day so that he would not die but would only struggle in pain and torture for eternity.

Chapter 8: Athena

The goddess of courage, inspiration, civilization, wisdom, and arts is Athena. Some identify her with Pallas Athene, and she is the protector of the city in an ancient Greek myth. She was created from Zeus' head and his forehead. She grew into a woman and helped Zeus defeat his father, Cronus. She also defeated the Titans led by Pallas Athene. Athena was provided with a shield and an Aegis.

In some myths, Athena is the daughter of Zeus. Some say that she was born from his head; others that she was taken from his forehead. Athena is one of the most famous female Greek deities. She was known as Tritogeneia ("born from the sea foam") at her birth.

She is considered as being one of the virgin goddesses. Athena became known to own gold, silver, bronze, truth, brightness (or wisdom), and justice, but she is also known to be a goddess who won over mortals.

Athena is the goddess of war and the city. Zeus created the goddess after he made war on his father, Cronus. When Athena was created, she had golden hair and a silver shield. She was the daughter of Aegis. She was the torch used in the sanctuaries for lighting the fire. She was also given the responsibility of guarding the gates of heaven and the underworld.

Athena is known to be a healer to people of all ages. This woman was given a gift that made her know all about life and death. People could ask for Athena's help as she would help them.

Hera, Zeus' wife, was very jealous of Athena because she had more power than Hera. When Athena came of age, Hera tried to kill her by locking her in a chest with a set of metal doors. The doors were all bolted shut except one, and when one door opened, it was Athena who let herself out. Athena left Hera for someone else. Athena and Hephaestus (the smith of the gods) had children together.

Athena's youth was divided into three parts. In her first part of life, she was good, honest, and kind. She worked hard to make things easier for her mother and father. In her second part of life, she started to work hard by devoting herself to art. She took great interest in art, especially music and dance. She is responsible for creating various instruments that made music more beautiful. During the third part of her life, she became a warrior. Athena is well-known for being the protector of the city. She is the goddess of wisdom, courage, and inspiration. Athena is the goddess of war and carries a shield of pure white. She also has a helmet with a goat's horn. She uses her wisdom to help protect the city.

Zeus fought against Cronus, and he used his Athena to defeat him. He threw her high into the air, and she landed on her feet with incredible accuracy. It is because of this that she became associated with war and protection. Athena's symbol is the owl. In Greek tradition, the owl is a symbol of wisdom as Athena's counterpart is the goddess of wisdom, Pallas Athene. The owl represents wisdom, olive trees represent peace, and spears represent her ability to be powerful in every situation. It is said that she looks over the city of Athens every night. She taught people how to make tools, work metals, and grow plants. Athena was also known for being a protector of her people.

Athena was once married to Hephaestus, but she turned him into a woman when he was sitting on Mount Olympus. He had been mating with Hera. Athena has two children with Hephaestus.

Chapter 9: Poseidon

Poseidon is a Greek god that rules over the sea and all water beings. He is the son of Cronus and Rhea, and as such, he is one of the Titans. This god has many children, such as Triton, Palaemon, and Polyphemus.

Poseidon has many powers. He can control storms, earthquakes, floods, tsunamis, and more. If people are too proud or arrogant, Poseidon sends them a flood to punish them for their sins, and we know from ancient history just how bad that can be. Poseidon is also the only god that rules over two kingdoms—the sea and the earth. It makes him very powerful since he creates earthquakes or storms when angry.

Since Poseidon is the sea ruler, he controls all sea creatures, including dolphins and other fish. He loves horses, and as a result, he is often depicted as a man on a chariot drawn by horses. Poseidon has many temples and altars dedicated to him. One of his most famous temples is located in Athens in an Acropolis area. It is one of the few ancient temples that are still standing today. The temple contains many sculptures that reflect Poseidon's power over storms and earthquakes.

Poseidon is one of the most popular gods in ancient Greece. Some people believe he is one of the most powerful gods and that he represents everything to the Greeks—the sea, earthquakes, and even storms. The word *Poseidon* means "king over the sea" so you can understand why he is so popular!

Poseidon is the son of Cronus and Rhea and, therefore, one of the Titans. He also has many siblings. The poet Hesiod describes him as being "the mightiest of them all" (*Theogony*) and tells us that he has a violent temper. This is shown by his killing his son Halirrhothius by striking him with a trident for an insult against Poseidon's wife, Amphitrite.

He married the goddess Amphitrite, and they had at least six children, one of whom was Triton, who is often depicted as a merman. He also had many other offspring.

In one story about Poseidon, Hera desired a golden apple tree given to her by Gaea as a wedding gift. When Heracles (Hercules) failed to get it for her because Atlas refused to give it up, she sent a storm upon Atlas' kingdom, which made him lose his strength and allowed Heracles to take the golden apple tree away from him.

Poseidon punished Heracles for his actions by sending a sea monster to attack him as he returned from the land of the Amazons with Hippolyta, Queen of the Amazons.

Heracles killed the beast but lost one of his fingers in the process (Apollodorus).

In another story which tells about Poseidon and Heracles, Hera forbade Hephaestus (Vulcan) his forge because he had sided with Zeus when Hera and Zeus were arguing. When Hephaestus returned to Olympus, Poseidon took him back to his underwater forge. There, Heracles found him and persuaded him to return to Olympus by offering him a reward. Heracles promised to help Hephaestus in any way possible. However, this was a ruse as the king of the gods wanted Hephaestus to return because he had made an unbreakable chain and wanted him to make one matching it. Heracles agreed to this but insisted that he would only create one if Hephaestus would come with him without any tricks (*Theogony*).

Poseidon was spoken of in many places in ancient Greece. For example, the Oracle at Delphi said of Poseidon often when he asked questions about the future. At Corinth, the Temple of Poseidon is a fundamental structure from ancient times and is still standing today. Many people visited it and offered sacrifices.

Aside from this, many ancient writers, such as Homer and Hesiod, wrote about him in their epic poems. These tales tell of his strength among the other gods. He was known as Pelagius by the Romans due to his patronage over naval affairs. He is also mentioned in several other mythological tales, but none is well-known as those mentioned above.

In 1928, an expedition was led to what is still known as the Poseidon Temple and found a statue of Poseidon in his chariot with the Greek alphabet and letters carved into his forehead. It was probably a reference to the story that tells of him causing the Greeks to write their names on their ships not to be killed by an avenging god!

The life of Poseidon is filled with many stories about him. However, most stories like this one do not support any common myths or ideas. Instead, they are more like stories that were used to teach specific moral lessons. Nevertheless, it is interesting to think about the differences between Greek and Roman mythology. For example, while Poseidon is generally portrayed more positively in Greek stories, he is shown in the Roman stories as less potent than many other gods. It is because Romans were influenced by cultures that worshipped a god called Neptune.

Poseidon is one of the most popular gods among ancient Greeks and Romans. He is also one of the most important gods and often represents natural disasters and destruction. His enemies include Uranus (the father), Cronus (the son), Hades (the brother), and Zeus (the son). He is also married to Amphitrite and has many children. The most famous of his children is Triton, the god of the sea.

Poseidon is the god of earthquakes, storms, and sea monsters. He is also believed to be responsible for bringing changes in human life, such as births, deaths, or major disasters like floods or famines. He is also associated with horses and chariots.

Chapter 10: Hera

Hera is the goddess of marriage and birth and, as the wife and sister of Zeus, the de facto queen of Olympus. Despite her title, ironically, the ancient Greeks knew her to be jealous and vengeful toward several of Zeus' lovers and children.

Hera was born to Cronus and Rhea and was the youngest of three daughters (after Hestia and Demeter). Her children were Ares, Enyo, Hebe, Hephaestus, Angelos, Eileithyia, and Eris.

Hera was so ancient that she probably predated Zeus. No one knows her real name either. "Hera" is, in fact, a title, translated as "lady" or "mistress."

Hera's rule over the heavens and earth preceded her marriage with Zeus; thus, many referred to her as the Queen of Heaven. Zeus himself was wary of her, for at any moment, she could lash out at anyone. Case in point: Hercules. Hera hated the illegitimate son of Zeus and the mortal Alcmene because of Hercules' adultery and a plethora of other character flaws. One time she raised a storm at sea to drive Hercules off course and, consequently, to kill him. When Hercules died, however, and was eventually taken to heaven, he and Hera reconciled.

Hera's marriage to Zeus was not a happy one. Zeus was cruel to everybody. Unable to bear any of that, Hera conspired with Poseidon, Athena, and a few other gods. She drugged Zeus, and they bound him on his bed and stole his thunderbolt. Thetis, however, summoned Briareus, and he untied Zeus.

Zeus was so consumed with fury that, with his own hands, he hung Hera in the clouds using golden chains and attached massive anvils to her feet. Hephaestus attempted to free her mother from such a degrading position. His will not to be questioned, Zeus banished Hephaestus from heaven, and the fall broke Hephaestus' leg.

Hera's vindictiveness did not end there, however. She once punished Io, one of the mortal lovers of Zeus, by having Argus take charge of her. Argus watched over Io to ensure Zeus would not come to her aid.

Hera also turned Calisto into a bear all because Zeus fell for her. Moreover, she arranged the death of Semele, yet another of Zeus' mortal love interests; however, it is worth noting that she did not directly cause it. Lastly, in many stories, Dionysus was torn to pieces because of her orders.

In spite of all these acts of jealousy and vengefulness (justified or otherwise), Hera has some redeeming qualities. She was the protector of women. She would often preside over marriages and birth. In the story "The Quest of the Golden Fleece," Hera was portrayed as an affable protector of heroes. Furthermore, her daughter Eileithyia was gracious enough to assist women in childbirth.

Although Hera was worshipped in virtually all parts of Greece, the locations of the temples erected in her honor were at Argos and Salmos.

Claims to her looks seem to vary—and at polar opposites at that. On one hand, she was described as cow-faced; on the other, she was called the most beautiful among the immortals.

Chapter 11: Artemis

The goddess Artemis is the Greek goddess of the hunt, wild animals, wilderness, childbirth, and fertility. She is a sister to Apollo and a twin sister to the god Hermes.

Artemis is depicted as a woman wearing a short dress with hunting boots, holding a bow in her hand as she walks gracefully over mountains or through forests and fields. As the goddess of hunting, she loved nature and would often roam alone through woods and fields. She would also lead her followers on deer hunts across these landscapes with torches burning brightly to find deer hiding in bushes or behind rocks. She is often depicted with her hunting dog named Orion. She later left these characteristics behind and became the goddess of childbirth and fertility.

The Athenians highly worshiped Artemis. In pre-classical times, she was known as a fertility goddess due to her nature, including the control of vegetation and animal life. She was more commonly known as Potnia Theron or Mistress of the Animals (Potnia meaning "mistress"). It is also believed that she would bless men with good fortune in the hunt in exchange for small sacrifices offered to her, usually in the form of animal parts, such as deer feet or animal skin. During this time, the deer was considered a sacred animal and one of her most important animal symbols. Later in the classical times, when she became more associated with the moon and other more powerful goddesses, such as Demeter, she began to take on their characteristics and became known as Artemis Agrotera or Artemis of the Wildland.

Artemis originated from Arcadia in central Greece, where her cult was based in a primitive religious community. This community focused on hero worship and was based around nature, wildlife, and fertility. She is often depicted with animals (including deer, bears, and wolves) and the moon and stars as symbols of fertility.

As mentioned, Artemis is seen as a long-haired maiden wearing a short dress in classical Greek art, hunting boots, and holding a bow in her hand. She is accompanied either by deer or hunting dogs, often with small torches to light up the darkness of forests and fields. As the goddess of childbirth, she is always depicted on vases holding a baby, also known as a foal. She is sometimes adorned with jewelry, such as gold pendants shaped like animals, representing fertility, life, or death.

Artemis was named after a celestial object in the night sky associated with the moon, known as the Pleiades, or "the seven sisters." Her name means "to shoot" or "she who shoots," which may refer to her role as a huntress or her role in childbirth and protection of children.

Artemis most commonly had companions that represented different aspects of nature. They included the following:

- Achilles: represented the seas.
- Apollo: represented beauty and harmony.
- Asphodel: represented death.
- Callisto: represented wild animals and hunting dogs.
- Coronis: represented birds such as doves.
- Cypselus: represented trees, vegetation, and seas.
- Deimos: represented stormy weather.
- Electra: represented wild animals.
- Euryale: represented wild animals, hunting dogs, seafaring, and childbirth.
- Hygieia: represented healing and the goddess of health (both mental and physical).
- Hylas: represented the moon and stars.
- Iris: represented the messenger of the gods with a rainbow-colored bow, known as Messenger of Artemis and Keeper of the Rainbow or Goddess of Rainbows because of her role in nature's

rainbow colors, such as red, orange, and yellow, which are associated with the moon.
- Luna: represented the moon and stars.
- Orion: represented the stars and is often depicted with Artemis in Greek art.
- Otus and Ephialtes: represented mountains.
- Peitho: represented persuasion.
- Poseidon: represented the sea.
- Silenus: represented old age, rebirth, wisdom, and drunkenness. He is known as the Keeper of the Nymphs because he protected young nymphs. He is also known as Wild Man of the Woods or simply the Wild Man because of his appearance, which referenced a beast-like creature that belonged to nature.
- Tityos: represented the earth and its fertility.
- Tyche: represented a fortune.
- Uranus: represented the heavens.
- Zephyrus: represented flowers, plants, seasonal change, and spring.

In animal form, Artemis is often depicted with a deer among other creatures, such as bees or butterflies, which symbolize rebirth and transformation (as seen in metamorphosis) due to its ability to go from a caterpillar into a butterfly when it becomes an adult. These creatures are associated with her because they can also be seen as wildlife or animals related to nature, which she loves so much in her role as the goddess of the hunt, wild animals, and fertility. She is also associated with such creatures as snakes, spiders, and peacocks.

Artemis is depicted in the stars. She is associated with many stars in the night sky, such as Orion. Her relationship with Apollo is seen in the stars when gazing upon a constellation of Orion. The seven sisters are seen in the Belt of Orion (the constellation), and Orion himself is known as the Hunter. His companion, Sirius or Agrotera, represents Artemis as she is known as the Huntress.

It was said that she was the daughter of (or at least had a close relationship with) Leto, the mother of Apollo and Artemis. She is depicted as having a sibling in Apollo, which is often coded as a brother because of his role as god of music. It can be seen in her appearance on vases that depict him alongside her.

Artemis is also depicted in Greek mythology as being born from a golden womb called Kybele (or Cybele). In later forms of Greek mythology, she is portrayed as being taken from the head of Zeus and named after him. The head of Zeus is said to be the seat of his mind and his will. She is also often depicted as having golden hair and wearing a crown made of gold on her head.

She is sometimes said to come from Mount Ida, which is associated with Leto, Kenta (a mountain in Crete), where she was born, or else from an orchard or garden on Mount Kallidromos (Mount Kallidromus). She is sometimes said to have been raised by the nymphs in a cave in Tanagra (Greece). It is also noted that she was raised by doves who fed her with honey from their beaks. These doves are said to have been sent by her mother, Rhea, to provide her this food.

Artemis is mentioned in several Greek myths, but she is not mentioned in the *Iliad* or the *Odyssey* because she is not particularly important. She is, however, mentioned in Hesiod's *Theogony* and Homer's *Hymn to Aphrodite*. Later stories tell about her birth, her conception, and her children. In Homer's *Hymn to Artemis*, she was born from Zeus' thigh after his wife, Leto, suffered through the pain of giving birth on land, which is where Artemis spent most of her time (on Mount Olympus).

Artemis' association with the moon persuaded many people to see her as a major goddess or equal to Aphrodite, the goddess of love and beauty. Some later

Greek writers believed that Artemis was a daughter of Zeus and that she was also a Titan.

Chapter 12: Achilles

Achilles is a hero from Greek mythology. His mother was Thetis, goddess of water. In the Trojan War, Achilles led the Myrmidons against Troy. He had a short temper and would often go into fits of rage when he did not get what he wanted, such as his captured prize, Briseis.

Achilles was seen as invulnerable because his mother, Thetis, dipped him into the River Styx to make him invincible while holding him by one foot. However, this only made his heel vulnerable to injury, and without it, Achilles could not defeat Paris in battle. Achilles was eventually killed by Paris using an arrow from the god Apollo while fighting at the front of the fight. Achilles' mother then put his body into a fire to burn away his mortal parts and to leave only his soul behind as an immortal.

Achilles is perhaps best known for being a central character in Homer's *Iliad*, which tells of Greece and Troy's Trojan War. In the *Iliad*, Achilles becomes enraged when Agamemnon, the Greek leader, takes a captive girl, Briseis, from him. Therefore, he refuses to fight until his friend Patroclus is killed by Hector. He had to battle after Patroclus's death. He kills Hector but is later killed himself by an arrow shot by Paris. The Greeks mourn over Achilles's body for 21 days until his father, Peleus, makes them give up the body. Peleus promises to bury Achilles with all due ceremony to calm them down. After their funeral service, the Greeks put the ashes of Achilles in a golden urn and place it next to his friend Patroclus' grave.

There are many different stories that are conflicted about his death. In the *Iliad*, he is killed by Paris, but the Trojans kill him in other versions. The Trojan War was later on turned into a spectacle and a game by the Roman poets. In Aeschylus' Achilleis, Achilles' death is depicted as suicide. He sees his friend Patroclus killed and pushes Patroclus's corpse into the river to make it look like Patroclus died from his wounds. Then Achilles puts on Patroclus' armor and pretends to be him. He is eventually killed by Hector but manages to wound the mortal with his fatal spear.

Achilles was a model soldier. He was a tough fighter but also very kind to the innocent people of the Trojan War. He and Patroclus were also close friends and brothers. Achilles was always willing to die for his friends, even if it meant that he would not live forever.

Achilles is the most famous hero in Greek mythology. There are many different versions of his death. Still, they all portray him as a great warrior and a strong-minded individual who showed fantastic patience in his anger and rage when people judge him unfairly.

Achilles is one of the most influential figures in Greek mythology; he is also one of the most famous. He led the Greek army against Troy at the less critical but epic battle known as the *Iliad*. This battle marked the beginning of the Trojan War, which continued for months. The main goal of this war was to capture Helen from her husband, Menelaus, and then take control of Troy. The Trojan War ended with a victory for Greece; this victory was known as "the fall of Troy."

The war was an epic battle with many known stories. These include the *Iliad*, which is a collection of poems by Homer, and the *Odyssey*, also written by Homer. These poems are two of the most famous works in Greek literature. The *Iliad* tells the story of the Trojan War in detail. The Trojan War is the most important story ever told because it ended in a victory for Greece and angered Troy's king, Priam.

Achilles was one of the essential warriors during this war; he was known as the best warrior of all time. With his help, the Greeks were able to defeat the Trojans. He was a magnificent warrior, but he was also a hero to all those who fought with him. Achilles was related to two women from the Greek army, Thetis and Agathe Tyche. Achilles' mother, Thetis is an immortal deity; she lived near the ocean because she loved it. She could control the wind and water with ease; she also had such a strong force of will that she could even control fate itself (even though Zeus created destiny). Helen was Achilles' sister; she was beautiful and caused many problems for everyone involved in this war.

Agathe Tyche is believed to be Achilles' wife in some sources. She was the goddess of fortune; she controlled all of the elements. She was also the goddess of luck, which she ruled with a dice game that she played with her husband, Eros. Agathe Tyche and Thetis came up with a clever plan to help Achilles; this plan showed how great these two women were by using their connections to help Achilles defeat Troy. They had Zeus make Achilles invulnerable for nine years during the Trojan War; he could not be hurt in any way. It meant that no matter what weapon a soldier used against Achilles, he would still be alive and sound at the end of the battle. The plan was set in motion when Paris stole Helen from Greece and took her back to Troy. The army of Greece then marched on Troy to get her back. When some Greeks found out Achilles was invulnerable, they decided to attack him, hoping they would hurt him. After Paris's brother Hector refused to fight Achilles, he called on his mother for help. She told him that he could kill Achilles if he used a magic arrow against him. Hector used it to try to kill his opponent. The hand was dipped in a poison that would destroy the object it hit, much like a snake's venom. It was only one arrow dipped in this poison, however, and it only killed Hector.

After Achilles was killed in battle during the war against Troy, his body was taken back to Greece and cremated on a pyre at Patroclus's grave. The Greeks had no idea how they would transport his body without harming it further; they were agitated because he had been their hero for so long and their champion during this war. The gods agreed that Achilles could live again on one condition. His mother, Thetis, would need to go to Mount Olympus and ask if they would allow a hero as great as him to live again. She had to ask for this favor for him to be brought back to life. Otherwise, he would stay dead forever. However, he was allowed to be brought back from the dead if someone would give their life in his place. Without another thought, his mother sacrificed her own life so he could come back and fight once more.

His mother's sacrifice so touched Achilles that he gave her his armor as a reminder of what she had done to help him. He also promised to give up fighting and live his life like a normal man, and he never broke this promise until the very end. Achilles falls in love with the beautiful but troublesome sea nymph, Thetis (his mother's sister), who would not let anyone be able to take her away from him. She said that she would only marry someone who was a brave warrior and would be willing to die for her on the battlefield, which is what Achilles was. Some say that Achilles's death was predicted by none other than Thetis when he was born. While he was spending time with his mother, some say that she gave him some prophecies about his future.

At the start of the story, Achilles is said to be very arrogant and proud of himself. He is a supreme warrior and wants to prove it to the world by making war with the Trojans. His first fight with a Trojan soldier goes well for him, and he does whatever he can to win it quickly without thinking about any repercussions or what would happen after that battle. He gets angry and frustrated when Paris, his best friend, refuses to fight him. The monster Scyllaeon, made of a sea serpent and dragon, threatens to kill him in front of his friends just so that he'll leave Thetis alone. However, Achilles is very brave about the situation and decides to face the creature single-handedly. He manages to defeat it by using its venom as a weapon against it. The monster almost kills him but is then killed by an arrow dipped in the poison of Polyxena's lasso (a type of rope used for capturing people). He becomes even angrier due to this incident because he hates anyone who uses his mother against his will. When he loses Patroclus, his best friend, he decides to break from the war and meet Thetis. Achilles ends up finding her and is reunited with her after not seeing her for a long time. He tells her about his troubles and says that if he doesn't die on the battlefield, he'll die soon because nothing will stop him from trying to be with her. Thetis tells him that she knew how it would end up, but she was willing to let it happen because they are connected by fate as mother and son; they can't stay away. She also tells him that she will always be there for him when he needs someone. Thetis informs Achilles that if he doesn't go back to war, the Greeks will lose. She also gives him a new set of armor that her father, Poseidon, made for him and tells him that she'll always love him no matter what happens. Achilles then returns to battle and kills Hector, the man who killed Patroclus. He gets injured by an arrow, which leads to his death because it was dipped in poison from Paris's lance. Some say that Thetis put this poison on his hand so that no one could hurt Achilles, and therefore, they are also saying that she is at fault for his death. The truth is that while she does love him and always will, she had to sacrifice herself to bring him back from the dead. The man who took his place was not as brave as Achilles, and therefore, he died after just one day. Some say that Achilles didn't die because of Paris's arrow, and some say that it's because of an act of bravery by another hero. The truth is that it was because of both. Another part of the story mentions how Achilles was trapped under a pile of bodies just to be killed. He was eventually killed by Hector but managed to wound the mortal with his fatal spear.

Chapter 13: Acteon

Acteon was a hunter who is most famous for being turned into a deer by the goddess Artemis to punish him for disobediently hunting on her sacred grounds. They say his hounds did not recognize him and tore him apart.

Many will think Acteon's story starts with his death at the hands of wild beasts, but this is not so. It starts earlier with his quest to capture the most beautiful animal in existence, Artemis's beloved deer. To find her beautiful quarry, he had to go onto her sacred territory. When he did so, he knew he risked disobeying Hera, Athena, and Artemis by entering their domains without permission from any of them.

Acteon was a son of King Ceyx of Trachis in Thessalia and a grandson of the hero Perseus. He is also related to many notable mythological characters. His mother was Althaia, youngest daughter of Calydon, Oeneus, and sister to Meleager. His maternal grandmother was Anaxo, the daughter of Phyllis. His great-grandmother was the Pleiad Asteria. His paternal grandmother on that side was Astydameia. There is also a possibility that Acteon was a son or grandson of Lycaon.

He expelled the Lapiths from Trachis and made himself master of their lands. As a great-grandson of Perseus, he was a relative of Heracles and counted among the Argonauts. His grandfather Ceyx had given a banquet to King Peleus and his son Telamon at the latter's marriage to the Ocean nymph Thetis, which all the immortals attended. Acteon was in attendance to witness the proceedings. When it came time for games and sacrifices, he brought as his prize an ox, which he offered to Phoebus Apollo, but Themis (or perhaps Prometheus) had warned Apollo that it would be better not to accept gifts from this man. He is said to have been one of those who shared the booty of Thebes, and he came to be a follower of Actaeon, who was nearly crucified with his dogs by Artemis. However, a sudden transformation saved him into a deer. He also accompanied Dionysus among the Argonauts and was present at King Theseus' funeral.

As a hunter, according to Hyginus, Actaeon fell in love with Diana (Artemis), but the goddess did not return his feelings, which enraged him so much he went hunting alone and killed her favorite doe. In revenge and at the prompting of Zeus, she changed him into a deer. Unable to walk on his hind legs and not knowing how to run like a deer, he was torn apart by his hounds. These hounds could not recognize their former master and became ferocious beasts that killed other animals; it was said that they were eventually turned into stone.

The gods punished Actaeon, a hunter (and son of Ceyx), by becoming an animal. He was hunted by the hounds of Artemis and turned into a deer.

Actaeon wrote many poems celebrating his hunting experiences. For example, "Sad he who, for the hunt alone, leaves his home."

A story told in *Aesop's Fables* calls for Actaeon's name to be erased from the list of heroes in certain cities (although it is not clear what these cities were or whether this is historically accurate). He did not see the hounds until they were shot at him, so when he was killed, he was not hunting and, therefore, did not deserve to be counted as a hero.

Another story tells how Actaeon followed Diana, who had revealed herself to him in a dream. He saw her one night bathing in Lethe's pool, but upon waking, he told his mother about this vision. She said that it must have been an illusion (Fable 19) and made sure that Actaeon didn't go any further with this hunt. However, he was determined to go on, so he searched for the pool to see the goddess and tell her that it was a dream.

MYTHOLOGY BOOKS FOR TEENS: LEGENDARY GODS AND HEROES

Late one night, when the moon had risen and Actaeon was about to follow her directions, his mother caught him in his bed. She said she didn't want him to die because of chasing after an illusion and that she would keep his father's hunting dogs always on their leashes.

Actaeon then took this as a warning from Artemis and fled from his home shortly after this conversation. He met with Heracles and asked him to help him find his quarry, but Heracles told him about the danger of hunting in Diana's domain. Actaeon asked Heracles to give him weapons to hunt with, but the hero refused and told him that he never went hunting without taking his father's hounds.

At this point in the story, Actaeon did not know of Heracles's hunting dogs. When he found them, the hounds recognized him, and they became fierce. When Heracles showed up, they attacked him as well; this is why Heracles could not hunt with his dogs. Actaeon's mother then started to lament for her son killed by a woman while following her orders. Artemis turned her lamentation into birds and her tears into a fountain.

A different version of Actaeon's death appears in Ovid's poem *Metamorphoses*. After seeing Artemis bathing naked in the spring, Actaeon boasted that he was more significant than the goddess and deserved to be worshiped more than she did. Enraged by his words that surpassed the limits of the divine, Artemis hunted down Actaeon as he was hunting that very day. She changed him into a deer, and his hunting dogs tore him apart. Apollo rescued his divine side in the form of a small shrub, which was then placed onto the Hyperborean mountain Lycaeus, where it blossomed into one of his sacred plants.

Chapter 14: Calypso

Calypso is a mythical island nymph in Homer's epic poem *Odyssey*. Although her myths are not consistent across different ancient sources, she is known for her captivating singing voice and was very reluctant to release Odysseus from his homeward journey.

What is Calypso?

The word *calypso* means "concealing," "hiding," and "protecting" in Greek, and Calypso was a sea nymph. She belonged to the race of Okeanids or Oceanids, one of the 3,000 daughters of Okeanos and his wife, Tethys, goddesses of earth's rivers and springs.

Okeanos was not only a river but also the god of the ocean. His wife, Tethys, had 3,000 daughters who gave birth to all beautiful sea creatures such as the Nereids, fifty sea nymphs.

Calypso was a mythical, elusive enchantress who lived on the magic isle of Ogygia, which Odysseus had to pass. Homer's epic poem *Odyssey* features Calypso. She was a very mysterious nymph who liked to hide in the cave. She would protect men from their destined fate as she did for Odysseus. He met her when he was traveling the ocean after the Trojan War. He strayed too far from his home, and crew members died one by one. Calypso was beautiful, and she promised Odysseus that she would release him if he spent a year with her. She lured him in with her enchanting voice, but she also preserved his life by keeping him for a year.

Calypso's cave was her mansion that was of great beauty. The walls were covered with gold, adorned with beautiful figures, and full of precious jewels. There were several caves full of treasure and entrances to the sea through other caves. All the inhabitants of that island were nymphs, animals, mythical beasts, and birds. They all had enchanting voices and speeds that any mortal man like Odysseus could not match.

He was a renowned hero who had sailed with him many times in the past. The island also had an oracle that told him about every possible future of people, but it would be a great sin to tell him about his future. Calypso did tell Odysseus about the reasons for keeping him in a cave instead of releasing him. The gods were angry with her because she had given Odysseus immortality, but she was defending her consort against them and protecting the travelers who came to visit her house.

Calypso was very sad because she was afraid that Odysseus would leave her island. She even tried to seduce him and offered him immortality, but he decided to obey the gods' will and left. She gave him a bag full of gifts and told Odysseus that he should close the bag when he passed by Circe.

Calypso kept Odysseus in her home for many years because she fell in love with this strong man. Her voice had magic powers that could charm anyone who heard it. Zeus and other gods also liked her voice.

Calypso belonged to a race of nymphs who are mentioned in Homer's *Iliad* and *Odyssey*. Even in Ogygia, where she lived, was associated with a particular mystical sound that could determine human behavior.

Chapter 15: Homer

Homer is often attributed as the celebrated author of the two great epics: the *Iliad* and *Odyssey*. These poems are written in a style of Greek that was considered to be spoken at an earlier time called Homeric Greek. He is also credited with writing these pieces based on legends and stories passed on by the last generations. These myths would narrate stories about famous heroes, gods, and goddesses like Zeus, Hera, Hades, Poseidon, Achilles, Odysseus, and Athena. All of these tales featured hallmarks such as honor without violence or concern for material wealth or family.

Homer is the earliest known poet. He was born in Ionia, and he served as a soldier in an army that fought against Troy during the ten-year Greek campaign, which is considered the first war in modern history. After completing his education, he was given to wear and became a highly respected hero who built up an extensive list of victories under him. One of his most notable battles was when he led his troops against Troy in war. It was at this time that Homer did two poems: the *Iliad* and *Odyssey*.

The *Iliad* told how the Greeks and Trojans engaged in a ten-year war to avenge a kidnapping that took place by

Paris. At one point, Achilles' anger got the best of him when he killed Hector, who would lead all the Trojans into battle. Before this incident could happen, Zeus intervened and made sure that Achilles wouldn't kill Hector before he had to fulfill an oath that he had sworn with his mother.

It is what led to the *Odyssey*. It told about how Odysseus spent many years trying to get back home after he was banished long before the events of the *Iliad* started where his men were fighting against Troy. The Odyssey showed how Odysseus and other heroes like him were made to survive in situations where they would have to face men who wanted to kill him or capture the ships. It also showed how he made it back home after experiencing heartbreak, battles, and many other kinds of ordeals.

Apart from being the author of these two poems, Homer may have been a blind man who looked after the education of young boys. There is another story that tells of how Homer was given a great honor from Alexander the Great. Alexander invited him to come from Greece to Italy to be honored with excellent writing, poetry, and prose skills.

The world of literature owes a great deal to this man. He was a poet who created the standards for writers who would follow him in his footsteps. Even today, these epics are still being immortalized in modern media like films and television shows.

Chapter 16: Odysseus

Odysseus is a figure out of Homer's *Iliad* and *Odyssey*. He is a Greek king of Ithaca who fought in the Trojan War. After ten years in Troy, Odysseus departs on his homecoming journey to find his kingdom conquered by the suitors. The suitors ignore Odysseus' warning and continue to live off Tyro's estate. They eat Odysseus' food without paying for it and sleep with her maids while she is absent.

Odysseus needs to take matters into his own hands on this mission; he has assembled an army and takes advantage of Helios-Apollo's distraction to sneak into Troy. The Greeks destroyed the city and stole away Achilles' remains after the battle.

This story revolves around the hero Odysseus' homecoming journey after ten years of fighting in Troy. After hearing about his old kingdom being trodden on by King Alkinoos' men, he seeks revenge against the Trojans. Within one year, however, he returns home to find that his wife, Queen Athena, and his son have died, and his kingdom is now under complete control of King Alkinoos. The only things left in Odysseus' old home are Helios-Apollo's chariot and a few blackbirds that act as messengers between him and Athena's spirit.

Odysseus' parents are Laertes and Antikleia. He was raised by the king, Alkinoos, in which he learned to be a vulgar and disrespectful individual, but at the same time, he also received much love from Alkinoos. He married Tyro after she had saved his life, and their marriage produced five children.

Odysseus is an essential character in the *Odyssey* because there would be no story to tell without him. The story is about him coming home to find his kingdom in ruin and the people he once cared about dead. His most notable characteristic is his considerable strength. Odysseus speaks "with the voice of a man twice ten men" (1.257), which is why he is so powerful. He also can kill gods like Ares, Zeus, Athena, and Apollo. Odysseus' strength and power also come from thinking on his feet. When Eumaios confronts him at the palace after pretending to be one of King Alkinoos' henchmen, he does not believe Eumaios until he sees the proof by Athena's chariot. The way out of a situation is not something Odysseus is afraid of, and he uses it often. One other characteristic that Odysseus has is his ability to lead others into victory. His incredible strength and unique speech make him one of the most powerful characters in the *Odyssey*, right behind Agamemnon.

Odysseus' wife, the Tyro, is a Trojan princess who was secured to him with a promise of marriage during the war against Agamemnon. When Odysseus returned from Troy, she revealed that she had not been faithful to him. As he departed again to win back his kingdom, he gave her gifts and made plans for her future. When he died, she found a letter from him with an oath to return if she needed help.

Tyro is a very sympathetic character because she is the object of Odysseus' affection in the story. Grief comes out when Athena tells him about her death and that his son has also tragically died. Tyro was not a very reliable character because she had affairs with many men, but she didn't deserve to die because of it. She was emotionally intense as she never told Odysseus about killing their son and how bad things were becoming in her kingdom, not to upset him or ruin his chances for success on his quest.

Tyro had many characteristics that caused her to stand out from other characters in the story, like how obedient she was to Athena's requests, even though they were not suitable for her. She helped Odysseus on his journey because she wanted to make sure that he would return alive. She was a very sympathetic character, and even though she had flaws, it didn't affect her sympathy.

Chapter 17: Tiresias

Tiresias is a figure in Greek mythology who was originally a man but experienced several transformations to different sexes. He is the son of Charles and the nymph Chariclo, granddaughter of Ares. Tiresias lived for seven years as an apprentice seer before making contact with two snakes while sacrificing on Mount Parnassus. The snakes are then revealed to be his grandparents, Apollo and Taygete, who transformed Tiresias into a woman as punishment for neglecting his duties as a priest. After nine years as a woman, Tiresias was bathing in a pool when he/she saw another pair of snakes. Tiresias was then transformed into a man, and he regained his sight.

Tiresias participated in the hunt for the Calydonian boar but was injured and blinded by one of the boar's bristles. The goddess Nemesis took pity on him and removed his sight and gave him the gift of prophecy, then recovered from his injury and continued to participate in hunts.

Tiresias was the son of Chariclo and the godly Laius. He was also said to be a brother to Leucippus (who was lame) and Arne. Tiresias, along with his brothers, was cursed by his mother, Chariclo, for sleeping with her and engaging with their father. In retaliation for beginning a relationship with another woman, he threw his spear at each brother in turn, all three falling from Mount Parnassus to their deaths.

Before becoming the king of Phrygia (his principal residence), Tiresias ruled the Larissae and the town of Larymna. Later, he became king of Illyria. When Icarus accidentally drowned in Lake Tritonis, it was said that Tiresias helped to heal his wounds and gave him a vision of his future family.

Tiresias was one of the Argonauts. He was a member of those who had visited the island in the golden liquid, which Phrixus and Helle had planted to prevent further war between their two countries. His son Astypalaea later became famous for proving that he could fly by building a pair of wings out of feathers sewn together and attaching them to his arms. The wings became too heavy to lift, and he fell to his death.

Tiresias foresaw the future in a dream at the wedding of Admetus, telling them that their son would kill him with a stone. He said to them that it was their daughter-in-law, Alcestis, who would make the final sacrifice for him after her death. It was fulfilled when Admetus' son died of grief at his mother's death.

Tiresias was given a crucial role in the war between the Phaiakes, who belonged to the minority Spartan faction, and the Athenians. He foretold that the Spartans would win during an assembly of both parties. The oracle's prediction came true after only a few days and a second time during an attack on Attica. Tiresias was killed after the Athenians took control of the oracle at Delphi.

After being killed, Tiresias was changed into a woman by Apollo and became a priestess of Hera in Cilician Thebe. He lived for many years before being transformed into an older man by Hera. Next, he has transformed into a woman again and became the lover of Teiresias (not to be confused with Ulysses' seer Teiresias), son of Eumelus. Teiresias had been turned into a woman by Apollo and was living in Cilicia.

Chapter 18: Oedipus

Oedipus is a Greek legend who has been told throughout history across many different civilizations. The story of Oedipus was first recorded in ancient Greek oral tradition and then transcribed into written by Sophocles.

Oedipus was born from Laius and Jocasta, the king and queen of Thebes. Zeus created a prophecy that children born from Laius would grow up to kill him one day. To prevent this from happening, Laius decided to have their son killed.

After this, Jocasta gave birth to a baby boy who was named Oedipus. He left Thebes in his youth and later became king of Thebes. After becoming the king of Thebes, Oedipus married Laius's widow, Jocasta, and had two children named Polyneices and Eteocles. When Oedipus came back from the war, he realized that his half-brothers were fighting over the throne of Thebes. So once again, he went out to war to stop them from fighting or killing each other. Once soldiers had defeated him in battle, they also killed their wives at the same time.

Oedipus then became distraught. He had killed his fathers and his uncle at the same time. He was terrified at what he had done, so he prayed to the gods to have them make him forget the past and the prophecy to save him from his destiny. The gods turned Zeus into a bull, and they left Oedipus blind so that he would not remember what had happened.

After losing his sight, Oedipus wandered throughout Corinth but was eventually found by a Corinthian king who took pity on him. As it turns out, the man was Laius, disguised because even blind men were terrified of being an outcast of society. The king took him to the palace and raised him as his own. When Oedipus grew up, he left Corinth and married his mother, Antigone. Because they were related by blood, she was also subject to the prophecy. They lived happily together until Oedipus' children were born.

Jocasta had given birth prematurely to Ismene and a boy named Eteocles. These first two children would turn out to be the ones destined to kill Laius, Oedipus' father, their grandfather, and king of Thebes, when they came of age. Once the first two children were born, Jocasta gave birth to a second son named Polyneices. He was a punishment sent from the gods for Oedipus having married his mother since he was destined to kill his brother Eteocles.

Oedipus became worried about the prophecy being fulfilled. After having children and knowing that they would kill their father and uncles, he exiled them from Thebes, in a far-away place where nobody knew them.

To put an end to the prophecy, Oedipus wanted to get rid of the children that were going to kill him. After banishing the first two siblings, Oedipus consulted Teiresias about having them killed by the servants, but he refused to do it for fear of being cursed as well. Teiresias knew that he couldn't handle seeing his children die and would be scared knowing what had happened, so he decided not to do it. As a result, he came up with another idea to have all of his offspring killed together, leaving him alone with Laius's son Theseus as his only child. When Oedipus found out that Theseus was his true son but had no idea who Polyneices and Eteocles were, he sent out some messengers to tell the two children to come to Thebes. Once they did this, led by Creon, the men Oedipus had sent murdered them both.

When it was later revealed that Creon had been the one who ordered their deaths, Oedipus started to become sick about this. He then concluded that he no longer wanted any of his sons to live anymore. He also ruled that the next king of Thebes could not have any children. It meant that no one else could carry on his lineage, and he would be able to keep his throne.

As Oedipus got older, he started questioning who Theseus' birth parents were but didn't want to know because it wouldn't make a difference since they were both dead anyway. He acknowledged that he had done wrong in the past and still wanted to perform better things for himself and his country.

Oedipus still felt incomplete because no matter how hard he tried, he couldn't stop thinking about Polyneices and Eteocles. Oedipus then decided that he would go to the place where Polyneices and Eteocles were buried. He didn't want to be reminded of how he murdered his children any more than he already was. He knew that Teiresias had put up a tomb at those burial grounds where the two brothers were buried with their mother and Thisbe when he found out the truth behind what happened between Theseus and Merope, the daughter of Creon.

Oedipus knew that the two were supposed to be together and would have a family. However, Oedipus was very unhappy with himself and couldn't see past his selfishness. He wanted revenge on Theseus for not being with Merope and for killing his sons. He tried to kill Theseus so he could then marry Merope himself. The darkest part of this whole thing is that it was all his own doing in the first place because he had convinced himself that Polyneices would kill him if he didn't do what they both needed to do to be together.

Oedipus decided to go ahead with his plan to kill Theseus. He comprehended that he was the only person who could do this and had no other option but to do it himself. After his sons' deaths, Oedipus had the men he had hired take Merope and put her up in a secret room. He then killed the servants that reminded him of Polyneices and Eteocles by having them be burned alive. It was out of pure anger and pride because he wanted to prove that he could have done what he wanted to do no matter what type of obstacles stood in his way by asking.

Oedipus ordered that Theseus and the people of Kerkyra be turned over to him. He then put Theseus' sons up as sacrifices in the locked rooms he had just had Merope put in. Oedipus then opened the doors where Polyneices and Eteocles were supposed to be buried. He saw their bones lying all over the room, which sent a chill down his spine. Oedipus was afraid of what he would find, so he put out a torch and closed the doors. The gates led out onto a bridge that was overlooking an area that was filled with water. The bridge was where his sons' bodies were supposed to be, but he instead saw the two men he had hired. He ordered his men to kill them, and they did. Oedipus was now the ruler of Thebes, but to keep

Diana's wrath away, he needed to sacrifice himself to win her favor and have an easy task when it came time for him to traverse Mount Olympus. Oedipus bluntly told one of his servants that he wanted to die and that he needed a place where nobody would see what was happening. He commanded his servants to build a funeral pyre for him on Mount Cithaeron. He was eventually burned on the mountain, and his ashes were then scattered.

While Oedipus was still alive, he found out that his youngest daughter, Merope, had slept with her husband and had been pregnant. When she gave birth to a baby that was not a son but a girl, Oedipus wanted to kill Merope and the baby, but Polybus managed to get them out of Thebes before Oedipus could have them killed. The baby had given into the care of servants while they were on their way out of the city for it not to be harmed. After they escaped, Merope gave the baby to a man she hardly knew in exchange for money. The baby was later passed into the care of a nurse and found refuge with her. The baby had been named Iope but had gone by Iocaste when she grew older until she discovered that her foster parents were not her real ones, and then she had taken a husband.

Chapter 19: Heracles

Hercules is a figure from Greek mythology, the son of Zeus. His name is probably cognate with Hebrew *Harkôs*, meaning "the one who has power." He was a paragon of masculinity, and his twelve labors would have been impossible for just one person to complete. Nevertheless, Hercules is not just some mythological character; he can be used as a model for writing your own self-development story.

Who is Hercules? Also called Heracles, Hercules is a Olympic-calendar hero in Greek myths whose number of exploits rival those of other gods. According to legend, he is from a race of divine heroes known as the Argonauts, who tried to complete Jason's quest for the Golden Fleece. According to *Thucydides*, he is the favorite and most powerful of the twelve labors imposed on him by Eurystheus, king of Mycenae, for his failure to find the cattle of Geryon.

Hercules began his labors at a very young age. When he was just a baby, monsters attacked his little brother Iphicles and Iphicles' wife, Alcmena. Hercules killed all their attackers quickly with his bare hands and saved them from death.

Hercules is known as Heracles (meaning "the brilliant one") to the Romans and Greeks because of his great strength, intelligence, skill, courage, and beauty. He is firm, with a chiseled body and arresting blue eyes. He is known for his incredible strength and can lift boulders and lions with his bare hands. He has superhuman stamina, so he would not get tired quickly from all the fighting and activity he had to do in many of his adventures. According to Greek mythology, Hercules is famous for having romances with many women except for his father Zeus' loved ones, such as Helen of Troy and Deianeira.

Hercules' name is derived from Greek *héracles*, which means "glory of Hera" (Hera being the queen of Olympus, wife of Zeus). When Hercules was born on Mount Olympus, his mother, the goddess Alcmene, forgot to make him immortal. Zeus, the father of Hercules, made his son immortal at birth.

Hercules or Heracles (referred to in the Greek myths) is a hero and a demi-god. He is part human and part god (a demi-god). The legends of Hercules are so old that many parts of them are lost today, but he is still considered one of the greatest heroes and most famous saviors of all time.

Hercules is so strong that he can lift a lion of nine cubs by the tail. Hercules would pull the lion through the city. After Hercules pulled the lion, he would release this animal and come running back to its family. It was an awe-inspiring feat because no creature could draw a nine-cub lion (even Hercules could not accomplish this feat).

Hercules fought many monsters. One of these was tested by Eurystheus, king of Mycenae, for his failure to find the cattle of Geryon. The beast was the Hydra, a nine-headed serpent. Hercules fought this creature alone and cut off each of its heads one by one with his sword.

Heracles is often shown in ancient art to be on the chest of Cypselus (c. 550 BCE) and in statues such as the famous Farnese Heracles (c. 290 BCE).

What were the labors of Hercules?

1. Slay the Nemean Lion.
2. Slay the Lernaean Hydra.
3. Capture the Golden Hind of Artemis and bring it back alive to Eurystheus.
4. Slay the Stymphalian Birds.
5. Capture the Cretan Bull sent by Poseidon to ravage Crete and bring it back alive, to be sacrificed to Hera as a peace offering, according

to Iphiclus' advice (who was sent by Eurystheus in place of Iolaus).

6. Take the apples of the Garden of Hesperides.
7. Slay the Arcadian Deer.
8. Capture the Erymanthian Boar.
9. Capture the horses of Diomedes, which were golden with bronze hooves.
10. Steal the girdle of Hippolyta, queen of the Amazons, and bring it back into Eurystheus' palace.
11. Obtain the cattle of Geryo.
12. Steal Cerberus from Hades.

One labor of Hercules that did not involve killing was done in a place called the Garden of Hesperides. It was a garden where the golden apples were kept. Hera placed these apples in the Garden of Hesperides. Hercules was supposed to pick them all up and return them to Eurystheus. Still, he ended up eating two apples himself, and Hera became very upset with him, so he could not enter Mount Olympus anymore. Some say that Hercules only performed one and not all of the labors.

What did Hercules have to do? He had to kill a lion. He had to capture the Hydra. He had to kill a bird and bring it back as a sacrifice. He had to capture the hind of Artemis and bring it back. He had to catch the bull sent by Poseidon and get it back as an offering to Hera. He captured the Stymphalian birds (twelve birds that would wake up whenever anybody came near them). He had to bring back the apples of the Garden of Hesperides that were guarded by Hera, who was a giant. He had to go back and steal Diomedes' golden horses that would run faster than any horse that had ever been ridden. He had to take the girdle of Hippolyta, the queen of the Amazons, kill her husband, and take it from his body.

Chapter 20: Medusa

Medusa was a Gorgon. The word *gorgon* means "dreadful." She had snakes for hair. According to the legend, she had once been excellent and was even more envious of the fairer goddesses than her sisters were. Consequently, Athena punished Medusa by turning her beautiful locks into snakes and making her face so hideous that she could turn people to stone just by looking at them with those eyes. Both in Greek mythology and art, Medusa's stare was said to petrify people. She was also called the Gorgon because she had a girl's face with the body of a monster. Her gaze could turn people to stone.

Medusa's gaze had been the cause of two deaths: That of Perseus and that of Andromeda. Only one man had ever been able to withstand her power, saving himself with a mirror. The myth was often used as an example of how women were not trusted, for it shows two instances where women are harmful to men.

Like all Gorgons, she had snakes for hair, and also she had serpents' tails for legs. She was terrible to look upon; she had a terrifying aspect, a face that no mortal could endure seeing.

Medusa was usually portrayed with serpents for legs. Originally, Medusa was described as beautiful but terrifying. She killed two men just by looking at them: Perseus and Minos. Only Perseus averted his gaze from her and prevented her from being turned into stone. In Medusa's most famous story, the hero Perseus beheaded her to rescue Andromeda.

The Gorgon's power lies in her gaze; however, if Medusa's gaze has harmed someone, they can avoid it by looking at their reflection in an object of some sort. In the battle against Perseus, Medusa laid eyes on him, but he avoided her gaze by looking at his reflection in a shield. Since he averted his gaze, he was able to cut off her head. He then used it as a weapon; wherever it fell, men would die, and women would turn into stones.

Medusa's face was later put on the shield of Athena herself; the head of Medusa is featured on Athena's shield. It symbolizes that even if someone sees Medusa, they will not be harmed by her gaze. It also alludes to Athena's apparent hatred for her; Athena reviles anything that is too beautiful or powerful (as she had been jealous of Medusa's beauty).

Medusa's story is one of the most famous in Greek mythology. The most important versions of the Medusa myth are those of Hesiod and Ovid. Hesiod tells us that Medusa was a beautiful woman with the hair of living snakes; she was once loved by a god who gave her a cap that made her invisible. She took advantage of this to watch Heracles as he performed his labors. In some versions, she turned men into stone with her gaze. However, Athena, the goddess of wisdom and knowledge, turned her into a creature with hair consisting of snakes instead. She was also given wings and the power to turn people to stone with her eyes. Ovid's version was quite different. In his version, Medusa was beautiful but jealous and resentful. She laid eyes on Perseus as he was performing his labors. In some versions, she laid eyes on him before he even did these labors. She rejected all his advances; therefore, she filled him with lustfulness, which caused him to fall in love with Andromeda. He turned himself into a dragon to attack Medusa, whom he killed by beheading her.

Chapter 21: Prometheus

Prometheus, from Greek mythology, is the Titan who stole and brought fire to humanity. This particular story is interesting because it has a twist. Prometheus gave fire to humans without asking for divine permission from Zeus. As a result, Zeus punished Prometheus by chaining him to a rock and sending fire-breathing eagles every day to eat his liver.

In one version of the story, Prometheus was punished by Zeus for giving fire to humanity. Prometheus snatched fire from the gods and yielded it to humans. Zeus, who did not want society to obtain such a dangerous power, chained him to a mountain as punishment. Every day, an eagle would appear and eat out his liver. The eagle was said to have been named after the Titan.

Prometheus is known for cleverly helping a man from the position of a thief rather than a benefactor or benefactors in this particular instance of cultural smuggling. Likewise, Prometheus in the Greek myth is associated with the creation of man. Prometheus is loved by Zeus and sent to earth to rule over men but is tricked by Zeus, who sends him a deceitful woman named Pandora. He opens the box, and all evil is released into the world. The only thing left in the box was hope.

In another version, he is married to Kora, daughter of Oceanus, and has a sister named Hesperis, who becomes his first love. In this version, he mates with the earth (Gaia), and from that union, humans are born.

In yet another version, Prometheus was chosen by Zeus to create the first human beings on earth from clay and water. After he does this, Zeus places some of his power and intelligence in them. He also puts a piece of his soul into them. As a result, they are not like the other people on earth who were created later out of the mud. They were superior to those and lived on Mount Olympus, where he placed them during the Golden Age of man.

Prometheus has several offspring. He is a son of Air and Earth, the brother of Atlas, Epimetheus, and Menoetius. In some accounts, he is the son of Oceanus and Tethys. In another version, he is a wild and unruly man named Cynortheus.

The myths mention him building the Titan's ladder to heaven. The seven gates of heaven are guarded by the Titans in their appointed places on Mount Olympos, but Prometheus steals fire from the gods who have put it there to warm them by its glow while they sleep. He gives this fire to humans for their protection and a way to live.

He is the creator of humanity whom he formed out of clay. He also created other things and invented helpful arts, such as sculpture, astronomy, navigation, medicine, mathematics, music, gymnastics, and many more skills.

He is known for creating the first race of men who were superior to those later made from mud who lived on Mount Olympus during the Golden Age because Prometheus had placed a piece of his soul in them. They were said to have been immortal and lived among the gods on Mount Olympus. Prometheus and Hephaestus built them.

Chapter 22: Minos

Minos was the son of Zeus. According to Greek mythology, he took over as king of Crete when his father retired to Mount Olympus. He married Pasiphaë, the daughter of Helios, and was succeeded by Icarus and Androgeus.

Minos had many children who were all murdered at birth by Minos's queen, Pasiphae (except for one). The notable exceptions are Ariadne and Phaedra. Minos had a close relationship with Poseidon; it was closer than that of most mortals. As king of Crete, his reign was so law-abiding that no murderer could escape justice. In retribution for the murder of his son, Androgens, Minos imprisoned those from Athens in a structure meant to hold only the worst criminals. It kept them as long as they were alive, but once they died, their spirits haunted the land, and their ghosts were an eternal shadow on any attempt to rule Athens properly.

The myth goes that the King of Athens, Aegeus, was told by an oracle that he must never let his son visit the land of the Minotaurs or else he would be killed. But one day, Theseus couldn't resist any longer and decided to go against his father. He went to find out what this whole Minotaur thing was all about. As soon as Theseus arrived at Crete, King Minos saw him and just knew he had to have him for a sacrifice. So Minos sent three of his bravest warriors to kidnap Theseus and bring him back to Crete to be sacrificed.

The Minotaur was a half-man and half-bull creature. Even though he was the son of King Minos, he was locked away in a maze for years to die of starvation or thirst. It is said that it took seven men to push down every wall that Daedalus made to put this magnificent maze together (Daedalus being the guy who built the labyrinth). Theseus set out to find this place at night to avoid being caught. It only had one way in and out. He also snuck a goat into his bag so it could bleat randomly, just like lost goats do. He snuck down the staircase and came around to find a considerable dog blocking his path to the labyrinth entrance. Theseus got very brave and formed an incredible plan to kill the dog. Then he continued, only to come across doors that were not meant for a mortal man like him. The doors were too small for a man. On one door, he found the image of a man with two mirrors coming out of it. He looked behind him but saw no one there. I mean, how could anyone be standing there with mirrors coming out of behind them? Then came another door that was empty as well but featured an owl hooting at night.

As he continued, he came across another door that said, "Abandon hope all ye who enter here." But Theseus had a motto of his own: "I fear no man." (It was not a fear-bucking motto but more of a challenge to the unknown.) So he entered through this door and eventually found himself in the middle of nowhere with no idea where he was going or what direction was left or right. However, he made it through alive and ran back to Athens as fast as he could because King Minos would surely try anything to get him back for good. And when he did get back to Athens, King Aegeus could not believe his eyes. He had given up hope that Theseus would ever return from his journey. Theseus told the king that he had killed the Minotaur and was sent a message in a wooden box to take to Athens for them to see. This is what the statement said: "Oh child of Aegeus, conqueror of the Minotaur and brave avenger of your friends' disgraceful death, go on doing such heroic acts. By their mark, you shall be known as an Athenian citizen, for you are owed an honor more significant than any other under this sun."

When King Aegeus read that, he was thrilled and proud beyond measure to have his son back, and they shared a grand reunion of father and son. Then Theseus became the king of Athens and made Aegeus the king of Piraeus (a seaside city in Athens where there is still a prison for criminals called Piraeus Prison). But even though these things happened after Theseus returned from his trip to Crete, some believe these events occurred before it.

Chapter 23: Orpheus

In his epic poem the *Odyssey*, Homer portrays Orpheus as a young man so gifted with music that he can charm people and beasts alike. He falls in love with Eurydice, but she dies from a snake bite during their marriage ceremony on their way to Hades' realm. He descends into Hades alone and charms Pluto and Persephone into letting him lead her back to the world of the living only if he does not look back to her until they have ascended from Hades together. Of course, he does turn around to see her. She becomes a shade again and is trapped in the underworld for all eternity.

Orpheus is part of a triad of ancient poets/musicians. Musaeus and Linus follow him. In ancient Greece, their names were often invoked at the beginning of an epic or the beginning of one of the Homeric hymns.

Orpheus is also often associated with Apollo due to similar interests. Although Orpheus is devoted to the Muses, Apollo also did work with them. Another connection between Orpheus and Apollo was the way that they both made use of music. Apollo played music on his kithara or lyre (depending on which version of the story you believe), whereas Orpheus could make trees burst into flower with his singing.

Orpheus was often depicted as carrying a lyre (a musical instrument), a bow, and an arrow. He held the lyre because he had been one of the nine Muses' pupils. According to legend, Orpheus was so skilled at playing his lyre that he could make animals and even trees follow his orders. The same music that he played would induce his listeners into a trance-like state. This power of persuasion is one of the reasons why Apollo wished to kill him.

Orpheus was initially a mortal. Born around 600 BCE as the son of the muse Calliope, he lived in Thrace (southeast Europe). His music brought him tremendous success, and he quickly earned a place among the Olympians at Mount Olympus. He even won the hand of his beautiful wife, Eurydice, by out-singing Apollo in a singing contest.

However, their marriage was doomed from the start. King Aristaeus wanted to marry Eurydice himself, and when she refused him, he became insanely jealous of Orpheus. On his wedding day, Aristaeus sent a horde of bees to sting Eurydice to death as she flitted innocently through a meadow.

Orpheus was devastated by her death and went on a quest to reunite with the love of his life in Hades (the underworld). Hades agreed to let Orpheus take Eurydice back on one condition: he had to walk ahead of her while traveling out of the underworld so that he would have time to turn around if she looked back at her former home. He agreed, and as he started on his journey toward Hades, he began to play his lyre.

But before long, Orpheus began playing louder and louder, forgetting that his beloved Eurydice was still behind him. Eurydice panicked when she heard the deep, mournful sound of her lover's music and turned to peek back at him. Just as she did so, she was immediately pulled into Hades forever.

Chapter 24: Daedalus

Daedalus was the son of the famous Athenian sculptor Eupalamus, who designed and built the wooden statue of Athena for the Acropolis. Daedalus is mainly known for being imprisoned on Crete with his son Icarus and fashioning wings made of feathers and wax so that they both could escape. However, Daedalus told his son not to fly too close to the sun because it would melt the wings. His warning proved futile when Icarus ignored this advice, and he fell into Mount Etna in Sicily and died while trying to escape from their imprisonment.

In the myth of Icarus, it is said that he was a handsome young man who lived in the sanctuary of Crete with his father, Daedalus. He was also known as Cretan because he was from there and had lived there all his life. The story tells how the gods were angry with Daedalus for creating a pair of wings for himself and his son, so they brought them to Sicily and forced them into exile on Crete as punishment. While they were exiled, Daedalus was given a vineyard but was not allowed to harvest the grapes because he had made wings for himself and his son.

One day, Daedalus visited his father's workshop in Athens. He saw a statue of a goddess on display there built for the city of Athens, and he remarked how beautiful it was compared to the figures that were already in place. His father replied by telling him about it, which explained how the goddess Athena was born from her mother's head without being created by a sculptor. "In the beginning, she was an idea," Daedalus said.

Since he loved his life in Crete, Daedalus longed to return to it. However, he did not want his son to grow up and face life without wings. So many years ago, when Cronus was king of the gods, Daedalus told his father that he would make wings for him and Icarus once they fled Crete to escape prison. He told Cronus that if they ever wanted their escape route back, they would have two choices: either sacrifice a prisoner every day or pay a yearly tribute of three birds as payment for their freedom. Cronus agreed to the terms and allowed them to escape.

So Daedalus and Icarus sailed south from Sicily, passing the island of Malta until they reached an island called Samothrace in the Aegean Sea. Since it was wintertime and they were making their journey in a small boat, they needed to pick up food along the way. While crossing an area of water called the Cretan Sea, Daedalus and Icarus saw an island in the distance that was barren of trees or vegetation. Thinking it would make for good farmland once they disembarked, they both made plans to land on its shores and build their homes there.

When they landed, the pair went to explore the island. After touring for a while, they came upon a cave and decided to go inside for shelter from winter. They found nothing but darkness in the cave, so they started a fire to give them light. Once it was big enough, Daedalus took some bronze and began kneading it. When he pressed his thumb into it, he discovered that there was gold mixed within it. He yelled out in surprise and was warned by Icarus not to shout because crying as loud as he did would surely draw attention to them. They decided not to go outside that night. Instead, they waited for morning and then left the cave with the intention of looking for food.

When they reached the shore, they found an abundance of fish and fruit that was growing there. They stayed with a fisherman who shared his home with them and taught Daedalus a way to make bread so he could feed Icarus. One day, when Daedalus was by himself, he took a walk through the forest, where he heard a voice calling out to him. He decided to follow it in hopes of finding whoever it belonged to until he came upon one of Cronus' ministers with whom he had shared his escape route many years ago. The minister told him that Cronus had forgiven Daedalus for fleeing Crete and that he was welcome to return as long as he could muster a tribute of one prisoner every year to be eaten by the Minotaur, a man-eating monster who lived in the Labyrinth.

Since Daedalus did not want his son to grow up and face life without wings and since his homeland had offered him a way out of bondage, he decided that he would take it. Daedalus asked his friend to tell Icarus what he had told him because he did not want him to know until he was ready for it.

So Daedalus returned to Crete to escape once again. The king welcomed him, and when he told him that he wanted to build a prison out of wood for his escape route, the king was pleased. "Go then," he said. "But you will need some assistance."

Daedalus was excited about building a wooden prison until he realized that it would not hold a prisoner forever. So he asked the king if there was any other way someone could be held in chains without being made of wood. The king told him that there was an island at the far end of Crete called Naxos where there lived men who had built great bronze traps to hold prisoners. So he sent Daedalus there to see if he could make a deal with them. When the two met, Daedalus told them how powerful

King Minos was and what he wanted to be done. They made an agreement that would provide them with a steady supply of prisoners for their traps in exchange for the friendship of Crete and her king and the knowledge of how to build their webs.

Chapter 25: Persephone and Hades

Hades, a son of Cronus and Rhea, is the god of the underworld. He rules over the dead—rather than all death in general, as the word *death* tends to connote in our world nowadays. In Olympian myth, he ruled over Tartarus with his brothers Zeus and Poseidon.

Hades had three sisters: Demeter (goddess of the harvest), Hestia (goddess of home hearth), and Hera (queen of Olympus). These four have a unique relationship: they are siblings but also lovers, mostly among each other.

Persephone, daughter of Demeter, was gathering flowers in a field when Hades came upon her and carried her away. Demeter searched the world for her daughter and finally discovered that Hades had taken Persephone to his palace under the earth. She went down to visit her daughter but could not persuade Hades to release Persephone. He gave Persephone pomegranate seeds to eat.

Obliging to divine etiquette but distressed at having Persephone taken from her and worried about what would happen next, Demeter asked Zeus to arrange for Persephone's release. Zeus agreed and sent Hermes to the underworld to get Persephone. He found her and freed her from Hades; he told Persephone not to pick the pomegranate seeds while she was in the underworld, or else she would be obliged to stay there.

Persephone returned to her mother but did not tell her what had happened. When the time came for Persephone to leave, she wept. Demeter, happy with her return, did not ask questions and told her daughter to pick a few pomegranate seeds on their way. Persephone obeyed the request and ate six seeds. However, she did not realize that she would be trapped there for six months of every year by eating the pomegranate seeds in the underworld.

When Demeter came to Olympus to get her daughter back, Hades and Persephone had been married for a while. Zeus suggested that the couple temporarily divide their time between Olympus and the underworld each year, but Hades refused since it would leave his kingdom unprotected. Demeter realized that if Persephone were allowed to live with Hades for six months, he would be obliged to release her. Zeus reluctantly agreed and allowed the couple to spend six months in each realm every year.

Persephone was required to spend one month with Hades each year. During her time with him, she rejoiced in the fertility of the earth and grasses. On the other hand, her mother had no power over the land during that time; she felt envy and sadness, mourning for her daughter's loss after being severed from her husband and her mother.

One day, Persephone was selecting flowers in a meadow when Hades came upon her and carried her away as usual. During their time apart, Persephone had dreamt that she was hunting in the underworld with the gods. Unable to eat anything from the land of the dead, she did not tell her mother of this dream and pretended to be happy.

While Hades and Persephone were visiting Zeus in Olympus one day, Zeus brought up her impending marriage to Adonis. She had consumed six pomegranate seeds during her time there and became obligated to spend six months each year with her father-in-law. Demeter believed that this would be a somewhat dull life for Persephone; she could not continue to live in such a joyless place like the underworld.

Chapter 26: Orpheus' Sibyl and Bacchus

The Late Antique summary of the *Bassarids* by Aeschylus tells how Orpheus disdained the worship of the gods except for the sun god Apollo. According to legends, he went out very early in the morning to Mount Pangaion to salute his god at the oracle of Dionysus. He was ripped to pieces by Thracian Maenads because he failed to honor Dionysus, his last patron. This story became the foundation of the speculation that the Orphic mystery cult regarded Orpheus as either parallel to or an incarnation of Dionysus. It's also interesting to note that a similar thing happened to Pentheus, who was also torn to shreds by the Maenads. Meanwhile, Pausanias wrote that Orpheus met his death at Dion and was buried in the same place. He added that when the women who killed Orpheus tried to wash off the bloodstain from their hands, the river Helicon sank underground.

Ovid also retells the story of Orpheus' death at the hands of the Ciconian women who were followers of Dionysus. In his account, Orpheus had abstained from the love of women for two possible reasons. The first reason is the death of his wife. The second reason is that perhaps he had sworn to do so. Feeling rejected with disdain and contempt, the women at first threw sticks and stones at

Orpheus as he played his instrument. However, they failed to hit him as the rocks, and the branches refused to hurt him as even they were charmed by the beautiful music Orpheus created. They can get their hands on him during the frenzy of the women's Bacchic orgies and tore him to pieces out of rage.

His lyre continued playing even at his death. His head, too, didn't stop singing mournful songs as it floated along with the lyre down the Hebrus River into the sea. The winds and the waves then carried them to the island called Lesbos, particularly the city of Methymna. The inhabitants of the place found his head and buried it, and they built a shrine near Antissa in his honor. His oracle was prophesied there and was only silenced by Apollo. His reputation spread because of the prophet, and people from Greece, Ionia, Aetolia, and Lesbos visited the place to consult the oracle.

Meanwhile, the Muses took Orpheus' lyre and carried it to heaven, placing it among the stars. The Muses also looked for fragments of his body, gathered them, and buried them below Mount Olympus at Leibertha. There, nightingales sang over the place where they buried him. When the river Sys flooded, the Macedonians carried his bones to Dion. Orpheus' soul then traveled to the fields of the Blessed in the underworld. There, he was finally reunited with the love of his life, Eurydice.

In another version of the story, it was said that Orpheus traveled to Aornum, an oracle for the dead located in Thesprotia, Epirus, hoping to make contact with his wife. Unable to do so, he eventually committed suicide. Finally, there's another account relating how Zeus instead struck Orpheus with lighting for lying about the mysteries and the stories of the gods.

Chapter 27: Mythological Creatures

Mythology is the study of myths. Myths are stories that have been passed through generations and cultures, though this does not make them any less accurate. Mythology is an exciting subject with many fascinating creatures and characters to study. Here is a list of some mythical creatures from Greek mythology:

- Harpies: In Greek myth, these are monstrous winged women who prey on the souls of sinners by seducing them to violence and death (though they weren't gods). Their name means "snatchers" or "terrorizers."
- Hippogriff: In Greek myth, these are winged horses with a human face.
- Kobold: These are malevolent forest spirits that haunted lonely travelers at night. They are almost always portrayed as ugly creatures like dwarves or trolls with an ax or a shabby tunic and boots.
- Lamia: In Greek myth, lamias are ghosts that carry off people's babies and devour their flesh. They are also known as succubi (female demons) though they are also considered the same as the incubus or succubus (a monster that visits sleeping women).

- Medusa: In Greek myth, Medusa is a beautiful woman with hair made of snakes. When she looks at someone, they turn to stone; however, Perseus is able to defeat her by using the head of a Gorgon (a female monster with fangs and a body made up of snakes).
- Minotaur: In Greek myth, the Minotaur is half-man, half-bull, and he is a monster born from the union of Themis (Greek Goddess of Law) and King Minos's son. He is half-human because his mother, Themis, gave birth to him while King Minos was still married to Queen Pasiphae, who gave birth after he divorced her. He was locked in the labyrinth built by Daedalus (a famous inventor and a son of Athena) at the Palace of Knossos.
- Nymph: In Greek myth, this is a spirit that inhabited a particular place and cared for nature. Though nymphs are spirits, some of them appear as humans or have some human features. They are also known to be the inspiration for most works of art.
- Sirens: In Greek mythology, sirens are half-bird and half-woman creatures that lure men to their deaths through seduction and song. Sirens live

on islands near Greece called Sirenum scapula (Siren Islands).

- Satyr: In Greek myth, this is a creature that is part-man and part-goat. Satyrs are usually depicted as playful and passionate creatures.
- Sphinx: In Greek myth, these are part-woman, part-lion creatures that guarded the city of Thebes. She would ask passing travelers a riddle but killed them if they couldn't answer it. Oidipous (Oedipus) was able to solve her puzzle by answering "man." When she killed herself afterward, he married her sister Jokasta (Jocasta).
- Triton: Tritons are a species of mermen found in Greek mythology. They are described as having a tail, fins on the legs, and webbed hands. They are half-human and half-fish.
- Valkyries: In Norse mythology, Valkyries are female spirits who would choose people to die in battle for their high rank or noble deeds. They also have certain powers, such as knowledge of fate or knowledge of future events.
- Vulcan: In Greek mythology, Vulcan is the god of fire. His father is Hephaestus (Greek god of fire), and his mother was Eileithyia (an ancient Greek goddess). Vulcan has many children, including the lesser gods and the classical gods

Heracles, Pan, Asclepius (the god of healing), Athena, and Apollo. He made weapons for the gods, such as thunderbolts for Zeus or arrows for Artemis. He also made shields for Ajax to protect him during battle. He created Mount Etna by striking a plague down on Sicily to make its people die and then burying them under it so that they wouldn't be able to come back to plague him again.

- Zelus: In Greek myth, this is the personification of zealousness or zeal. It can take a human form, influence people, and make them do things against their will.

Below are common monsters and heroes in Greek mythology:

- Demi-god: These are half human and half god, such as Hercules.
- Cyclops: These are the one-eyed giants that ate humans, like Polyphemus and Odysseus.
- Giants: These are large creatures with superhuman strength, such as Antaeus.
- Healers: They can restore someone to health no matter what condition they were in. Some well-

known healers are Asclepius (god of medicine) and Hygieia (daughter of Asclepius).

- Prophets: They interpret omens that are delivered by gods to humans on earth. Examples of prophets are Cassandra or Calchas.
- Priestesses: These are women who sacrifice themselves to their gods, such as Hecate.
- Medusa: Medusa was a Gorgon whose gaze turned people to stone.
- Mermaids: They are beautiful humans or beautiful creatures that lived underwater, such as Nausicaa, who was found by Odysseus, and Achilles' mistress, Polyxena.
- Emperors: These are the people in charge of the government, like Zeus and Poseidon.
- Witches: They are women who perform magical tasks, like Circe.
- Fairies: These are small human-like winged creatures, such as Chiron, that cause trouble for humans.
- Gnomes: These are fairies known for their knowledge and skills in music, such as Orpheus or Apollo's son Aristaeus.
- Sirens: They are half-bird and half-woman creatures that lured sailors to their death with their beautiful voices.

- Centaurs: These are half-human and half-horse, such as Chiron and the horse that was ridden by Bellerophon.
- Centaurs that were part of the Pan's army in Thebes: These consisted of all types of centaurs, such as those that wore shields. They were led by Inachos, the son of Priam and Hecuba.
- Shepherdesses: Women who tended flocks or herds, such as Atys (whose murder led to the Trojan War).
- Satyrs and Nymphs: They are the companions of Dionysus (god of wine).
- Chaonian Polyphetes: This is a mythical figure from Boeotia who was a fisherman who stole the cattle of Dionysus.
- Nymphs: They are the female characters of Greek mythology who lived near water and trees, such as Dryope.
- Amazons: These are mortal women warriors with superhuman strength, such as Penthesilea.
- Old Man of the Sea: This is a monster that Odysseus fought on his way home from Troy.
- Gorgon: Medusa was a Gorgon whose gaze turned people to stone.

- Kings and queens: These people are the rulers of the kingdom, such as King Augeas and King Admete (or King Demeter).
- Rhamphorhynchus: These are winged creatures that are the size of humans, such as the Rhamphorhynchus of Lake Bolbe.
- Folk gods: These are mortals that were worshiped in their area, such as Pan.

Chapter 28: Vikings or Norse Mythology

What Is a Nordic Myth?

Nordic mythology is one of the best known in the world. Explore the Viking cosmology and get to know a few of their favorite deities through these six legends.

The worlds of Nordic mythology are abundant with gods, giants, and strange creatures. No matter where you look, you will find an adventure waiting to be explored. But what is a Nordic myth?

Nordic myths stem from the Northern European Germanic traditions, which had a rich oral tradition filled with stories about gods, giants, and heroes. These tales were eventually written down in the thirteenth century as sagas translated into many languages.

Why Were the Vikings Important?

The Vikings left a lasting impression on European history, but why were they so important? Whether you want to relive the thrill of raids, learn about their deep roots in Norse mythology, or just understand the past, here's everything you need to know about these famous raiders.

In Norse mythology, the Vikings believed that the world would end in Ragnarök. They believed that the gods would die off and everything would fade into nothingness. Not all of them thought the world would rise again or that the world would be reborn better and more beautiful. Many scholars have debunked the version of the mythology, which states that a newer, better world was reborn. They say that the addition of that part of the story to the mythology came after Christianity arrived in Scandinavia. They say Christianity influenced Norse mythology and diluted it. A researcher and storyteller, Daniel McCoy, wrote that the rebirth addition came only from three late sources, one of which was dependent on the other two. Simultaneously, all last mentions of Ragnarok speak only of the destruction and never of any rebirth.

What did Ragnarök mean for the Vikings back then?

Imagine that you are living in a world where you knew everything was doomed anyway, no matter what you did. Imagine that the supreme beings in which you believed, the gods you prayed to, had limited powers and could do nothing to stop the impending doom. How would you live your life?

In many religions of the world today, when the world ends, there is some sort of blissful afterlife excellent and faithful people go to when they die. But this does not happen in Norse mythology—at least not in the older version of it.

If you lived in such a world where everything was going to be destroyed eventually, and the very gods you served were going to perish with it, and not even the memory of anything that ever existed would be saved, how would it affect your way of life? Would it cast a dark shadow over your life? The utter senselessness and hopelessness and futility of it all would surely bother you. Perhaps, this is indeed how the Vikings perceived the world.

However, Ragnarok may also have had other meanings for them. Even though the knowledge that everything is doomed is depressing, it may have given them a realistic view of their existence. The prophecy of doom didn't need to make them completely hopeless. The promise of Ragnarok also inspired them. In essence, since the gods were all going to die one day, humans too would die as well, and it was fair that both gods and man would face the same fate. If gods could go out and meet their future with dignity, honor, and courage, so could human beings. Thus, the Vikings believed the inevitability of death and misfortune should not just discourage or depress humans but should instead spur humanity to uphold noble attitudes and do good deeds—the kind worthy of being serving as praiseworthy legacies for us even long after we are gone.

What Is the Concept of a Viking God and Goddess?

The Eddas, Norse sources on Viking myths, refer to both male and female gods. Sometimes these are known as Vanir or Aesir deities.

It is thought that the various goddesses represent different aspects of women, such as fertility and masculinity. The goddess Freya is often depicted as a messenger between humans and the gods, sometimes even leading souls into Valhalla. Some legends say she was also once married to Odin, but she cheated on him with Loki. When Odin found out, he put a curse on her to forget everything that she slept with a man. Odin became her husband after she gave birth to the sons of Suttungr.

In the stories of some gods, they have gone to war against one another, and in other cases, they have assisted each other. There is also a story in which they argue amongst themselves on who is the most powerful.

As with many mythologies, there are various accounts of Norse mythology. There are references to an afterlife and hell in some stories, while this was not so in others. Some tales of gods fighting giants also represent conflicts between the Aesir and Vanir. As we can see, Norse mythology is rich and complex; it involves many different characters spread out over many generations of deities and their offspring.

When Did the Viking Myth Start?

Many myths are surrounding Viking history, from the current popular favorites to the children's tales. One of the most enduring legends is King Arthur, who supposedly traveled to Iceland and Britain to fight a mighty battle with a terrifying red-headed villain. Not only is this story not true (though there are many fascinating historical truths behind it), but it's no match for the Viking myth, which can be traced back thousands of years ago to Scandinavia.

Some of the most exciting myths concerning Vikings are the creation myths. The most famous of these is Thor's fishing trip, in which he enlisted the help of a giant to construct a net (with weights on the bottom) and catch three young whales as bait for a great white whale. To calm the waters so that he could do this, Thor had to row his wife, Sif, out into the ocean and kiss her, which accounts for why she has hair made out of gold in a myth with no gold objects. Some other creation myths, such as the tale of the origin of agriculture in Scandinavia, account for wildness and lack of civilization.

In many situations, Viking mythology reflects their society (and provides us with insights into their culture). We know that Vikings had a rigid social structure in which everyone knew his proper place. A woman could not bear arms. Only men were permitted to marry. Inheritance went from father to son. Additionally, they believed that the souls of people who died on the battlefield passed into a misty realm known as Hel. From there, they arrived before Odin's great hall and were judged for their time spent in Hel. Unjustly slain warriors were allowed to return and fight alongside the gods, while just people enjoyed eternal peace in Asgard. Within these myths lies an explanation for the Viking's love of combat and their desire to dominate.

Chapter 29: Aesir Gods and Asynjur Goddesses

Aesir gods and Asynjur goddesses are an essential part of Norse mythology. They are frequently the focus of the stories, but their roles are not always clear.

The Aesir are the main gods of the Norse pantheon. They consist of the following gods: Odin, Frigg, Thor, and Freyja. The Aesir are also referred to as Æsir, which is similar to the Latin word *dei*, which means "gods."

The Asynjur are female gods in the Norse pantheon. They are the daughters and wives of the Aesir. Some of them are: Freya, Skadi (Skade), Idun, and Nanna. The Asynjur are also referred to as Asyn or Asyn, which is similar to the English word *ashen*, which means "ashlike." The goddesses Idun and Nanna were thought of as rulers of the apples in Odin's hall because they were never eaten (Idun) or turned into an apple tree (Nanna).

Below is a list of Aesir gods and Asynjur goddesses.

- Odin: As the leader of the Aesir gods, Odin is a primary focus of Norse mythology. He was initially an Asynjur goddess named Alfrigg but was later transformed into an Aesir god. He is called All-Father because he is the creator god and protector of humankind.

- Thor: He is the son of Odin and protects Midgard (middle earth) from giants and monsters. In some stories, he also guards Asgard (home of the Aesir gods) against specific threats. Thor is also known for his mighty hammer Mjölnir, which he uses to fight giants named Þrymr.

- Loki: He is a significant figure in Norse mythology. He is involved in many stories, both heroic and treacherous. Loki is the father of Fenris (wolf), Jormungandr (the Midgard Serpent), and Hel (goddess of the underworld).

- Baldur: His parents are Odin and Frigg. He is a very nice god and is loved by everyone in Asgard except Loki, who seeks to kill him because of their disagreement. His wife is Nanna, the daughter of Njord.

- Tyr: His parents are Odin and Frigg. In one story, Loki cuts off Tyr's hand to make the Aesir gods think he was a traitor. However, Tyr became a god of justice after this and was known for his clever judgments.

- Heimdallr: He is the watchman of the Aesir gods. He stands on the Bifrost Bridge, which is the rainbow that connects Midgard to Asgard. He can see for three hundred miles in every direction (including into Hel). He is also the son of Odin and Bestla (daughter of Bor).

- Frigg: She is the wife of Odin. She is the goddess who oversees the well-being of the Aesir gods, which means she makes sure everything goes smoothly. Frigg is also known to be very kind and helpful toward others.
- Freya: She is a goddess from Freyja's clan who is not very friendly to her sister at first. Freya is one of the three Norns in Norse mythology who created everything that exists and gave humans their lifespans. She's also known for her beauty and is often seen as the most beautiful of the Norns.

Chapter 30: Thor: The God of Thunder

Thor is a Norse god in Norse mythology. His hammer, Mjölnir, creates lightning when it hits the ground, and Thor helps battle frost giants and jötnar wearing his belt. A hearty debate still goes on over the gender of this deity, owing to grammatical gender in Old Norse potentially being epicene, but Thor is generally regarded as male.

Thor is the eldest son of Jörð, the giantess, and Odin. He is the protector of both Asgard and Midgard. He constantly battles the giants who attempt to bring harm to these realms.

In Norse mythology, this sturdy, bearded god has a significant presence. In Old Norse, he is known as Þórr and Donar in Old High German. Thor is the god of thunderstorms, war, and fertility. He glides through the skies with his goat-drawn chariot (the two goats were named Tanngnjóstr and Tanngrisni), his hammer Mjolnir, his iron glove, and his magic belt—all of which are his most valued possessions.

The Story behind Thor's Hammer

Thor's hammer has always been an iconic part of his identity for many different groups of people. It is because he wielded Mjölnir in battle. He would use it to help him confront enemies.

According to the sagas, Thor's hammer was lost when he became unconscious from a migraine. Sif went to find it. She took the hammer and hid it so that she could return it to her brother's possession. Thor had then floated away into space for nine days and nights while his family searched for him. Sif eventually found out where he was and visited him there, at which time they were both invited by Odin, king of Asgard, to see his palace together (Thor was a bit upset that he wasn't invited). Thor was then given his hammer as a gift for saving the world. At this point, it is said that the hammer became sentient after having been submerged in water (a possible reference to Norse myths about giants and hammers, which were ruined by a flood).

The hammer's thirst for blood was quenched when Thor smashed King Heimdall's eyes out during an argument, destroying them forever. The loss of his eyes led to Heimdall no longer being needed by the gods and was instead placed in charge of watching over the rainbow bridge, Bifröst. It is where the concept of Ragnarok originated.

Thor's hammer was lost again when he fell into a vat of ale. His younger brother, Loki, took it and hid it with the dwarves. The hammer was again found by Odin, who retrieved it from the dwarves through subterfuge. The attempt failed when Thor threw his hammer at King Heimdall, who also sought to slay his wife inside the castle walls. The throw was so powerful that it broke the barrier and caused it to collapse.

Years later, Thor once again lost his hammer when he went to a feast at Utgarda-Loki's castle and was challenged by the inhabitants. Loki went to find Mjölnir and pretended that he had won it from Thor in a contest where he had thrown an ordinary-looking stone at Thor's head. Mjölnir then flew back to his hand, which left everyone at the feast in awe of its abilities. Loki then took the hammer and hid it with the dwarves.

The last time Mjölnir was lost, it was again stolen by Loki. While this was happening, Thor traveled to Hel, where he found himself trapped in a dead-end. He pleaded with his father Odin to free him to go back and make things right for his blind brother, Loki. Odin agreed on one condition: that Thor brings back the goddess Freyja as a bride for himself. Freyja was asleep in a cave, so Thor wrestled her out and got her back to Asgard. Freyja then made the mistake of falling in love with Thor, sending Odin into fits of jealousy. She was forced to leave for Hel, where she would have her time with the dead.

The true identity of Thor's hammer has been debated since Old Norse times. Mjölnir is said to mean "fist swing." This name can also be understood to mean "the earth's jewel."

Thor's Journey to Asgard

Loki told Thor that there was a king in Etinhome called Outgarth Loki, who said that the Etins of Outgarth were stronger than Thor himself. "That's something we'll have to see," said Thor. He set off straight away with his goats and his wagon, and Loki went with him as his guide. They rode through the skies, and the thunder rang out around them.

That evening, they came to a farmer's house, where they stayed for the night. The farmer was called Egil, and he lived there with his wife and two children (a boy called Thialfi and a girl called Roeskva).

It was a poor farm, and there wasn't much food to go around. So Thor took his two goats, Tooth Grinder and Tooth Gnasher, and slaughtered them both. He flayed the skins from the goats and set the meat to boil in a pot on the fire. When it was done, Thor carefully spread the coats on the ground away from the fire.

Thor and his friend sat down to eat, and he asked the farmer and his family to join them for supper. "Come and eat with me," he said, "and share my food. But take care of the bones, and lay them on the skins here."

They all thanked Thor and sat down to eat. The farmer and the farmer's wife, the two children, and Loki ate one of the goats, and Thor had the other one. Loki saw that Thialfi had a thigh bone in his hands. He had eaten the meat, and now he was turning the bone over in his hands, thinking of the tasty marrow inside.

Loki leaned over and said, "Thor won't let you eat that. Look how much he's keeping for himself. He's eating a whole goat while we all have to make do with one between us."

Then Thialfi got a good grip on the bone, split it open with his knife, and scooped out the marrow. He put the bone down on the skin with the others.

Thor slept there that night, and in the darkness, before dawn, he got up and dressed. He went over to where the bones were lying in heaps on the goatskins, away from the embers of the fire. Then he took out his hammer, and he raised it over the bones to bless them.

The two goats sprang up alive and well, and Thor petted their heads and stroked their backs, but he found that one of them had a broken leg.

Thor frowned. "One of you has broken your word to me," he said, "and broke the bone of one of my goats."

You can guess how scared the farmer was when he saw Thor's brows sink over his eyes. When he saw the look in Thor's eyes, he thought he would drop down dead with sheer fright. Thor's fist was clenched so tightly round his hammer that his knuckles were white.

The farmer and his family cried out and begged for mercy. He fell to his knees and said, "Please spare us! We'll give you anything you want."

When Thor saw how scared they were, his anger left him, and he calmed down. But as payment, he took their children, Thialfi and Roeskva, from them. They became Thor's servants, and they have followed him ever since.

Thor was keen to get on with his trip to Outgarth, but he couldn't go in his wagon because his goat was lame. So he left his goats at Egil's farm and set off for Etinhome on foot.

He took Loki and Thialfi with him, and they walked to the sea. Then he set out over the deepest ocean, and when he came to land, he went ashore. They hadn't gone far when they arrived at the woods, and they walked all day through it. They made good progress. Thialfi was the fastest of lads, and he carried Thor's bag with their food in it, but they didn't know where they were going to stay that night.

They were still looking for somewhere to stay when it was getting dark. After a while, Thor and Loki found an empty house with a wide-open doorway that stretched from one side to another. They went inside and settled down to sleep, but in the middle of the night, they were woken by a terrible rumbling. The ground under them was shaking, and the building shuddered with the noise.

Thor got up and looked around. He found that there were long thin rooms at the back of the house, and there was also a shorter side-room where Loki and Thialfi could lie down. Thor sat up in the doorway and kept watch, with his hammer ready in his hand. They heard terrible groans and rumblings all night long.

When daylight came, Thor looked out and saw someone lying nearby in the woods, and he was not small. He was sound asleep and was snoring loudly. And every time this giant snored, the ground shook, and the trees shuddered.

Then Thor knew what the noises had been in the night. He settled on his belt of strength and took up his hammer, meaning to finish him right away, but just then, the giant woke up and sprang to his feet.

"Who are you?" said Thor.

"My name is Skrymir," he said, "but I don't need to ask your name; I can see you're the god Thor. Have you been in my glove?"

Skrymir swept out and picked up his glove, and then Thor saw that he had used it to stay the night in and that the side-room where Loki and Thialfi had slept was the thumb of the glove.

Thor was just wondering how he could get rid of Skrymir when the Etin asked, "Shall I come with you and have your company?"

Then Skrymir undid his knapsack and started to eat his breakfast. Thor and his friends went a little way off to have their breakfast by themselves.

"Let's put all our food together in one bag," said Skrymir.

"Okay," said Thor.

Skrymir put all their food in his bag, tied it up, and slung it on his back. They walked all day, and the Eetin took great strides so that Thor had to run to keep up.

In the evening, he took them to a giant oak tree. "We'll stop here and rest for the night," he said, "I'm ready for bed myself, but you take the bag and get yourselves some supper."

Skrymir stretched himself out on the ground and fell fast asleep, and the branches of that oak tree were soon shaking with the sound of his snores.

Thor picked up the bag and started to untie the knot. But no matter how hard he tried, the knot just got tighter. When Thor was getting nowhere and got angry, he seized his hammer Miller in both hands, stepped up to Skrymir, and knocked him on the head.

Skrymir opened one eye. "Did a leaf just fall on me, Thor?" he asked. "I guess you'll have eaten by now, and you'll be ready for your beds."

"Okay," said Thor. "We're just on our way to bed now."

Thor and his men went off to another oak and settled down to rest, but they couldn't sleep. In the middle of the night, when Skrymir was snoring so loud that the whole forest rumbled, Thor got up and swung his hammer down hard on Skrymir's head. It was dark, but he felt it sink right into the Etin's skull.

Just then, Skrymir looked up and said, "What was that now? Did an acorn fall on me? And what are you doing, Thor? It's not time to be up already, is it?"

"No," said Thor, stepping back quickly. "I just woke up. It's the middle of the night. It's still time to sleep." But he thought to himself that if he got another chance to hit that Etin, Skrymir would never open his eyes again.

A little before dawn, he heard Skrymir snoring. Thor jumped up and swung his hammer with all his strength at Skrymir's head so that it sank in right up to the handle.

Skrymir sat up and rubbed his head, saying, "There must be some birds awake up above me. I'm sure something fell on my head from the branches just now and woke me. Are you up already, Thor? It must be time to get going now, I suppose."

"Yah," said Thor.

"Don't worry. There's not far to go now before you get to Outgarth," said Skrymir. "But listen! If you do get to Outgarth, you'll see some big lads there. So don't act up because Outgarth-Loki's men won't put up any nonsense from little lads like you. You can still turn back and go home. But if you're sure you want to go on, then you'll have to go east. My road goes north, through the mountains."

Skrymir picked up the bag and slung it over his back. Then he set off into the woods. The gods didn't say they hoped to see him soon.

Thor and his men went on till about midday when they saw walls of Outgarth on the plain in front of them; they had to crane their necks to see over the top. The gate was shut, so Thor went up and tried to open it.

They struggled with the gate for some time, and they couldn't get it to open, but then they found they could squeeze through between the bars. Inside the stronghold, they saw a great hall. The door was open, and they walked inside.

Sif

Sif is a goddess associated with earth. The Prose Edda records that she is the wife of Thor and that together they have a son named Ullr. The god Loki sometimes becomes Sif's husband when he takes the form of a mare to seduce her.

Sif is mainly known for her role in Norse mythology as a goddess associated with earth. It made her the wife of

Thor and mother of Ullr. Her hair was the golden color of sunshine/yellow gold. She wears a golden necklace known as Brisingamen, an ornate pendant consisting of a band of alternating clusters of oval and circular links strung together on a cord or chain.

Because Sif's hair is said to be the color of sunshine/gold, some people believe that she is related to sun goddesses such as Dana. Sif's hair color and clothing are similar in description to other goddesses such as Freyja, the Vanir goddess of beauty and fertility.

Sif is also the goddess of love in Norse mythology. Her name means "love" or "affection." Brisingamen is a gift from four dwarfs who loved her (the dwarves being Dvalin, Alfrik, Berling, and Grer). It was said to be made from gold gathered from all parts of the world by Asgard's roots.

Sif's Golden Hair

Sif is the wife of Odin's hot-tempered son Thor. She is magnificent, and her greatest glory is her golden hair, which gleamed like living sunlight. But one day, Loki saw her sleeping, and on an impulse, he crept up to her and shaved her head. Sif woke, discovered her baldness, and was both furious and ashamed. Thor was angry. He thought Loki the likeliest one to have done such a mean and pointless thing, and he stormed into where Loki sat and promised to break every bone in Loki's body. Loki didn't deny Thor's accusation but thought that it was a price too high to pay for a joke. He told Thor that no lasting harm had been done and then swore a binding oath that he would soon restore Sif's hair to its former beauty. As soon as Thor let him go, Loki hurried to the dwarf brothers Sindre and Brok and asked them if they could forge beautiful golden hair that would take root and grow in the head of a living woman. It is not recorded that Loki offered to pay them or that he did deliver them. These dwarves, it seems, took delight in their work for its own sake. They made the hair that Loki requested, and they created two other wonders for Loki to present to the gods. One was a spear that would never miss its mark. The other was a ship made with such enchantments that it would always have a favorable wind, and the greatest wonder about that ship was that, when not needed, it could be folded like a napkin and kept in the ship owner's pocket.

Perhaps the sight of such treasures made Loki greedy. Maybe the dwarves' skill made Loki jealous, and he wanted to provoke them. Whatever his reasons, he told them that surely they would never be able to produce such wonders again. They took offense at that. Loki took it a step further, wagering his head against Brok's that they could not make three treasures even more wondrous than the first. Now Brok was the assistant, not the master-smith himself, but his confidence in his brother was absolute, and he took up the wager.

Sindre accepted the challenge his brother had set. He put a pigskin in the furnace and told Brok to work the bellows steadily, never letting up, or else the work would be spoiled. Brok set to work, but as he did, a fly settled on his hand and bit him hard. He ignored the pain and kept at the bellows until Sindre returned to open the furnace—and out stepped a shining boar with bristles of gold. Sindre then placed gold in the furnace and went away, leaving his brother the exact instructions as before. Brok blew the bellows faithfully, although the fly returned and gave him a deeper and more painful bite on his neck, which throbbed ever more fiercely as the furnace blazed hotter. Sindre pulled a gold ring from the stove, threw some iron in, and told his brother once again to work the bellows with absolutely no hesitation, lest the last and greatest of his works should turn out to be worthless. Brok set to work again, but the fly came back, and this time it stung his eyelids so that the blood flowed down and blinded him. Brok stopped the bellows for a moment so he could swat the fly away, and the fly, which seemed to have a solid sense of self-preservation, took itself off and stopped troubling him. But when Sindre came back for the last time, he was angry with Brok, saying that Brok's interruption had nearly spoiled the work. He drew out a heavy and robust hammer with an unfortunately short handle, apparently satisfied by Brok's distraction.

Loki was waiting at the smithy door in his shape, and if he had in the meantime been the fly that tormented Brok, neither Sindre nor Brok could prove it, then or later. Brok took the treasures his brother had made, and he and Loki journeyed back to Asgard together. Side by side, they stood before the assembly, explained the wager, and showed the treasures. Three gods were appointed to receive and judge the gifts: Odin, Thor, and the god Frey, Freya's brother.

Loki gave Thor the golden hair (which rooted itself in Sif's head and grew splendidly), and Thor saw no more need to break all his bones. Loki gave Odin the spear that never missed its mark and Frey the folding ship whose sails could fill with the wonder-wind and bear it swiftly wherever Frey desired. And the gods marveled and were glad.

Then Brok stepped forward with the second set of gifts. He gave the golden boar to Frey, explaining that it could run as fast as the very best of horses. He also said that it could run over the waves of the sea and the winds of the sky as though they were solid ground and that it would shine and cast light about it even in the deepest darkness. To Odin, he gave a ring, explaining that it would produce eight other rounds every ninth night as heavy as itself. And he gave the iron hammer to Thor, saying it could strike the hardest thing in the world without being harmed, would never miss its mark when thrown, and would always return to its maker's hand. He also said that at Thor's word, the hammer would shrink to a tiny thing easy to conceal in the folds of his clothing. Brok ruefully acknowledged that the hammer had one fault—its handle was relatively too short.

The gods admired the beauty and perfection of the other gifts, but they judged that the flawed gift, the short-handled hammer, was the best of them all because it could be used to significant effect against the frost giants. Brok, therefore, had won his wager.

Loki, alarmed, offered to give costly gifts to keep his head on his shoulders. But Brok—perhaps remembering the biting of the fly—said he wanted nothing but Loki's head. "Take it, then," Loki said, leaping away. For Loki had a treasure of his own—shoes that let him run swift and light over the air and the sea. Brok, who had no such thing, could not catch him. Brok demanded that Thor bring him back, and Thor—perhaps grateful for his gifts, possibly wanting to avoid dishonor for the gods, maybe still angry with Loki about Sif's hair—chased Loki, caught him, and hauled him back before Brok and the court of the gods.

Loki didn't beg—not that it would have done him any good. Instead, he said that Brok had won his head, well and good, but the wager had said nothing about his neck, and if Brok couldn't remove his head without spoiling his neck, then Brok would have to go home empty-handed. Brok, incensed, summoned an awl from the air, boring holes in Loki's lips, and sewed his mouth shut before Loki could think of a legal objection. None of the gods seem to have objected to this either—perhaps because most of them had suffered from Loki's taunts, his lies, and his dangerous advice. Nevertheless, Loki managed somehow or other to get his lips unsewn, for his perilous words come up in many stories from a later time.

The Giants

Norse mythology has three core groups of deities. The Aesir, the Vanir, and the Jotuns. The Aesir are those who live in Asgard (god realm). The Vanir are deities who live with Freyja in Vanaheim (goddess realm). And lastly, the Jotuns are giants that dwell under Ymir's frosty body and are killed by Odin and his brothers.

The giants often get a bad rap as brutish creatures slain by Odin and his brothers at Ragnarok because they refused to do work for him or serve him in any way. However, they also get a bad rap because they—while not divine—do have their own will and very much do worship Odin. There is even an instance where a giant gives Odin help in some stories to defeat another giant.

Ymir

The first giant to be mentioned in Norse mythology is Ymir. He was born from the primal waters and was the father of all the giants. Ymir lived for a long time and had two children, Skirnir and Finari. The gods noticed that Ymir's body was rotting away, so they decided to kill him by bringing his body down to earth and stoning it. Once it fell from the sky, his blood fell and made the ground wet, forming the ocean giant Týr.

His flesh fell and made the earth; his bones became rocks and stones, his hair trees, and his skull the sky. The gods then took Ymir's eyebrow hairs and made Midgard (the earth). They found two trees: an ash tree with lights called Askr (ash) and an elm called Embla (elm) that they brought life to by carving faces into them.

A man was then created from the tree Askr, a woman from Embla. The man was named Ask and woman Embla, who then multiplied to form men who inhabited Midgard.

According to Norse mythology, the gods were not happy with Ymir's giants, so they decided to kill them. One day Loki went to Gymer's (fire giant) house and killed his son. When Gymer found out what happened, he took Loki and put him in jail.

Then all the gods had a meeting and decided that they would have to create more people. The gods would make them, but the frost giants would kill them. So Odin went into Jotunheim (home of the frost giants) and asked for a female giant named Bestla, who had been married to a frost giant called Buri.

Odin asked for her hand in marriage, and she agreed. She was the daughter of Bure and Urda. Odin, Bestla, and their son named Odin had three sons named Vili, Ve, and Tror.

Together Odin and his two brothers killed Ymir, the frost giant. They threw his body into a cave that formed the sea. Then they created Midgard from his body by making the earth from his flesh, rocks from his bones, mountains from his teeth, trees from his hair. His skull was made into heaven (Norse mythology). The stars were made from sparks from Muspelheim, a volcanic region.

Then Loki, who had been released from jail by his sons, went to Asgard (home of the gods) and killed the watchman of the gods named Heimdall. Heimdall was then reborn as a small child and later became king of the Slavs. The gods then knew they needed to rebuild Asgard, so they did it with bricks made from Ymir's teeth. They also created Ása-Ligha (giant tree), which is why trees can be so tall today.

Idunn and the Apples of Youth

There is a legend about Idunn, the goddess of youth. After the great battle between the Æsir and Vanir on the plain of Vigrid, Idunn was with her husband, Bragi, on a rock when they saw Sigyn come to take their son Bragi away from them. Sigyn swooped down on them with a mother's concern, and despite Bragi's pleas that she wait until they had finished grieving at least for some time before taking their son from them, she grasped him in her arms and flew away.

As the lamenting couple turned away, a falcon flew from the heavens and landed beside them upon seeing the two gods. The falcon addressed them with kindness and sympathy, saying that Njördr, Freyja's husband, sent it. Njord had appealed to all the other gods to watch over Bragi and Idunn until their son would be old enough for old age to claim him.

Rising into the air, the falcon spread its wings and took flight in pursuit of the mother and her son. Far ahead of them, he could see Sigyn flying with her prey. He fled after her so fast that the air whistled around him. At last, catching up with her, he struck at her breast with his beak and drove his claws into her flesh. She struggled in pain, but the falcon grabbed Bragi and flew away to a remote place where neither gods nor men could find them.

Sigyn had fallen to the ground with a heavy thud. She now sat on the earth, still clutching her son's hand as she mourned for him. The falcon came to them once more, flying down low over their heads and spreading his wings in a sign of protection over mother and child. Sigyn begged him to save her son, but he passed away, saying that this was not the time of the gods to interfere in human affairs, as it were when they were first created.

Idunn should go home and prepare for her son's reawakening in the spring. Then he would be brought back to Asgard and become a god among the Æsir. Sigyn wept, and as she did so, her tears fell onto Idunn's lap.

She looked at the golden bough in her hand and remembered how she had gathered it and brought it down to earth. She thought of the apples in Aegir's garden, the source of life kept safe for the gods. She had promised to protect them for all time, and now Sigyn was weeping because her son was taken from her.

The golden bough in her hand was covered with buds and flowering twigs from which a fragrant perfume arose. Idunn thought that if she could take them to Asgard, everyone would be young again. She leaned forward and plucked a twig from the branch when suddenly a white bird appeared on its tip. It perched there, shaking its wings and singing so sweetly that it seemed the song was being played on a harp.

The bird told Idunn that the branch was now dead and she should leave it alone. The buds had opened, and they were full of seeds that she could scatter everywhere over the earth to make fruit grow everywhere. She understood then that this was what she must do—scatter the seeds of youth over all the world.

Idunn gathered up her load of golden twigs and went home to Asgard. There she gave an apple to each god, sparing no one else but Hödr, Baldr's blind brother. As he ate the apple, he became young, his sight returned, and he joined the gods once more. Idunn then scattered the seeds of youth over all the worlds.

Hermóðr

Hermóðr is the son of Odin and brother of Baldr. He rode to Niflhel after Baldr's death to plead for his return. After Baldr was killed, the gods carried his body to the sea. They placed Baldr's body on a giant ship. The gods summoned the troll woman Hyrrokkin to perform Baldr's funeral ceremony. She came riding in on a wolf, using vipers as reins.

The gods placed food, golden cups of mead, and many other precious items on the ship with Baldr. Horses, dogs, and birds were carried on it, too. Odin laid his unique ring, Draupnir, on the pyre. When Nanna saw this, her heart burst with sorrow. She died instantly of heartbreak, and so the gods placed her on the ship next to Baldr to rest in peace.

Thor lifted the troll woman Hyrrokkin onto the ship and said, "I see beyond the threshold. I see into Niflheim, the world of the dead. There I see my kin, and I see Baldr seated in the great hall, feasting with his brother, reunited and at peace with each other at last." Hyrrokkin cut the head off a rooster, which had a body as dark as soot and neck as red as blood. She threw the chair away and placed its body in the boat. With that, Hyrrokkin lit the ship on fire. Soon, it was engulfed in flames. It was how a Norse funeral was held, and the gods thought to themselves, Baldr will have an incredible journey to Niflheim.

But Frigg was not ready to say goodbye to her son, no matter how peaceful his journey. She wanted him back. So she asked her youngest son, Hermoder the Bold, to go to Hel on her behalf to offer a ransom and return with the brothers. Odin brought out his horse, the eight-legged stallion, Sleipnir, and said to Hermoder, "Here, my boy. It is time to ride across the dewy mountains, through the ogres' lands, to Hel. I'll give you my horse to carry you over the dark, flickering flames, through the deep valleys of death."

Hermoder spoke to Sleipnir, "Carry us across the world and through the darkness, and let us return, or I fear that we shall both become victims of that mean old ogress Hel." Then they galloped away.

Hermoder rode for nine nights through deep and dark valleys. He saw no stars, no moon, and no sun for all that time. Finally, he came to the river Gjoll and crossed a golden bridge. On the other side, the guardian of the bridge, Modgud, was awaiting him. "Who are you?" she asked. "The other day, a whole army of bloody warriors with ice in their hair and beards rode over this bridge, but the bridge trembles more under your horse's hoofs. You do not look like you're dead."

Hermoder replied, "Indeed, I am not dead. Frigg and Odin have sent me to barter with Hel. I am going to retrieve my brother Baldr from Niflheim."

Modgud nodded and told him, "Baldr passed the river Gjoll and rode over the golden bridge not so long ago. You will have to ride toward the north and then down to find Nagrind, the gates of Hel."

Hermoder rode on. When he reached the gates of Hel, they were so high and icy that he could not pass. He performed Odin's galdr (song magic) and awoke a Valkyrie (war goddess) named Sigrdrifa. The Valkyrie rose from the ground and said, "I've slept for long. I've slumbered too much. Great are the misfortunes of men. Odin is the reason that I could not break the sleep. He covered me with shields in Skati's Grove and lit the enemy of wood on fire around my hall in a blaze, and told the warrior to cross it. He told the fearless to wake me from my sleep. The fine spoiler of gold came to me. He alone is better than all the others, a Danish Viking in the army! Come now, Hermoder, and I shall lead you to Hel. Take my hand, and we shall cross to Niflheim."

Hermoder knew that this Valkyrie would help him. Together, they went through Nagrand, the gates of Hel, and into the courtyard. In the land of the dead, Hermoder saw many awful things: skeletons and ghosts, ghouls, and mortal men. He and Sigrdrifa walked along a river filled with swords and spears, axes, and all kinds of weaponry. "This is the river Slith," Sigrdrifa told him. "It will burst out of Niflheim someday when the world is destroyed."

They walked for a long time and then they entered a great hall. Hermoder looked to the left and then to the right. He saw benches made of iron, and sitting on them were many Draugar—the undead, the ghosts. At the end of the hall, he saw Hel on her throne. Beside her were Geirrod, the evil ogre king, and his two daughters, Gjalp and Greip. Geirrod had a big iron rod sticking out from his chest, and his daughters' backs were broken from a battle they'd had with Thor long ago.

On the walls in Hel's hall, there were beautiful drinking horns, shields, and weapons. Hermoder was impressed with their splendor, but Sigrdrifa said, "Don't touch them. If you do, you will have to stay here forever. Don't take anything that Hel offers you because then you won't escape with your life."

Hermoder approached Hel. In front of her sat Hanginkjapta, an ogress with a broken jaw that hung down to her chest. Hanginkjapta spoke for Hel. First, she offered Hermoder a drink of mead, but remembering Sigrdrifa's advice, he declined. Then the servant Ganglot came toward him, her left foot broken and dragging along the floor. She offered him some food. Hermoder saw that the food was rotten and moldy and declined.

Then, Hermoder saw Baldr and his love Nanna seated in thrones across from the ogre king Geirrod. Hermoder fell to his knee and begged Hel to let them go. She did not move, but her voice came roaring from the mouth of Hanginkjapta: "If all objects in the world, alive and dead, weep for Baldr, then he will return to the gods. But if one thing, alive or dead, refuses to weep, then he will stay here."

Hermoder was dismissed. Baldr and Nanna followed him out of the hall, but they stopped outside. As long as they remained dead, they could not go any further. As a token to remember him, Baldr gave Hermoder a ring, Draupnir, to return to Odin. Now that Draupnir had been to Niflheim, it would drip and produce a new golden ring every ninth night. Nanna gave Hermoder a swan cloak for Frigg and a golden call for Fulla, and then they parted ways.

Sigrdrifa guided Hermoder safely back to Nagrand, but he could not pass through the gate when they got there. So Sigrdrifa took a rooster that had a blood-red neck and soot-dark body, cut its head off, and threw it over the gate. Immediately, Hermoder heard a rooster croaking on the other side, and sunlight shone through the mist. In an instant, he was back in the world of the living.

Hermoder rode home to Asgard and told the gods what Hel had said—that when everyone and everything wept for Baldr, he would be released. Upon hearing this, Frigg and her twelve maidens flew across the world as swans for days and days and asked all things, dead and alive, to weep for Baldr. Everyone agreed except for a single troll.

Chapter 31: Baldr's Death in the Twilight of the Gods

This story begins when Baldr, the good, dreamed big dreams and saw harbingers of danger to his life. When he told the Æsir about these dreams, they gathered at the council. It was decided to demand, for Baldr, a guarantee of safety from every kind of damage.

Frigg got oaths that everything would be safe for Baldr: fire and water, iron and every kind of metal, stones, earth, trees, disease, animals, birds, poison, and snakes. And this was done and defined. It was a pastime for Baldr and the Æsir that, while he stood upright, all the others aimed at him, some from far away, some from close by, hitting him, some hurling stones. Whatever was done, nothing hurt him, and to all of them, it seemed a great advantage.

But when Loki saw this, he was sorry that nothing would harm Baldr. Taking the form of a woman, he went to Frigg. Frigg asked the woman if she knew what the Æsir had done.

Then Frigg said, "Neither weapon nor wood can harm Baldr. All things have sworn me in."

Loki then asked, "Have all things sworn to spare Baldr?"

Frigg replied, "A small plant grows to the west of the Valhöll, which has the mistletoe. I thought it was too young to demand an oath."

Immediately afterward, the woman left. Loki took the mistletoe seedling, tore it up, and went to the Æsir. There Höðr was alone outside the circle of others, for he was blind.

Loki said to him, "Why don't you throw something on Baldr?"

He replied, "Because I don't see where Baldr is and also because I am without weapons."

Loki said, "Do as others do. Honor Baldr. I will show you where he is. Hit him with this stick."

Höðr took the mistletoe and threw it at Baldr according to Loki's directions. The blow pierced him and knocked him to the ground, and this has been the greatest misfortune among the gods and men.

When Baldr lay dead, all the gods were voiceless, and so the hands stretched to catch him fell back. They looked at each other, and everyone had a single thought against the one who had taken that action. But no one could take revenge. So sacred was that place of peace.

And when the Æsir tried to speak, they were instead crying in the throat so that no one could express their pain to the others. Odin suffered this evil more than any other because he knew better than anyone what significant loss and damage they suffered in Baldr's death.

When the gods returned to their senses, Frigg spoke and asked who among the Æsir wanted to earn all his love and benevolence by walking the road to Hel to see if he could find Baldr and offer Hel a ransom in exchange for allowing Baldr to go home to Asgard. Hermóðr the Bold, son of Odin, volunteered for this trip. He took Sleipnir, the horse of Odin. The Æsir took Baldr's body and brought him to the sea.

The ship of Baldr was called Hringhorni. It was the largest of all ships. The gods wanted to use it to travel to Baldr's pyre. However, the ship did not move.

The giantess named Hyrrokkin from Jötunheimr summoned. She came upon a wolf and had poisonous snakes for reins. She stepped down from her mount, and Odin summoned four berserkers to guard that mount. They couldn't help but knock it over.

Then Hyrrokkin stood against the ship's bow and, at the first push, moved it so that the fire came out of the supports and the lands trembled. Then Thor grabbed the hammer and would have smashed her head if the gods had not interceded to spare her. Then the body of Baldr was brought to the ship. He saw his wife, Nanna, daughter of Nep. Her heart was torn with grief, and she died. Also, she was placed on the pyre, which was set on fire.

Thor was present and consecrated the pyre with Mjölnir. However, a dwarf named Lítr came running to him. Thor kicked him and made him end up in the fire, where he burned.

At this cremation ceremony, people of various lineages intervened. Primarily, it was Odin. With him came Frigg and the Valkyries and his ravens. Freyr arrived on the wagon pulled by the boar named Gullinbursti or Slidrugtanni. Heimdallr straddled Gulltoppr while Freyja drove her cats. A great crowd of giants also came.

Odin placed at stake the gold ring called Draupnir. It was its nature that, on every ninth night, eight gold rings of equal weight detached from it as it dropped. Baldr's horse was led to the stake with all the harnesses.

It is said that Hermóðr rode nine nights in valleys so dark and deep that he could see nothing before him until he reached the river Gjöll. Then he galloped over the bridge above it. It was covered with shining gold. Móðguðr was the virgin who looked at the bridge. She asked him for her name and her lineage and said that they had crossed the bridge with five groups of dead men the day before. "But the bridge is not less beneath you alone, and then you do not have the color of dead men: Why to go the way of Hel, thou?"

He replied, "I will ride to Hel to find Baldr. Did you see Baldr on the way to Hel?"

She said that Baldr had crossed the bridge of Gjöll there, and down the north was the road to Hel. Then Hermóðr rode until he reached the gates of Hel. There he dismounted, secured the harness, climbed back, and gave a spur. The steed leaped with such impetus over the gates that he certainly did not even touch them.

Then Hermóðr rode to the hall and got off his horse. He entered the hall and saw Baldr, his brother, sitting on the highest seat. Hermóðr spent the night there.

In the morning, Hermóðr asked Hel to tell him that Baldr was going home with him and said how great the pain was among the Æsir.

But Hel replied that this was the occasion on which it would be possible to prove whether Baldr was so universally loved as was said. "If all things in the worlds, living and dead, will mourn him, then he will return to the Æsir. However, he will remain at Hel if someone refuses to do it and doesn't want to cry."

Then Hermóðr got up. Baldr took him out of the room. He took the Draupnir ring and sent it to Odin as a souvenir. Nanna sent Frigg a cloth and other gifts, including a gold ring for Fulla. Then Hermóðr retraced his steps on horseback and returned to Asgard, where he reported all the facts that he had seen and heard. Immediately, the Æsir sent messengers worldwide to ask that Baldr be wept over and, thus, taken away from Hel. And they all did—men and every other living being and the earth and the stones and trees and every metal. As you will have seen, these things cry when they come out of the frost and into heat.

When the messengers returned home, having done their job well, they found an older woman sitting in a dwelling. Her name was Þökk. They also begged her to cry about Baldr to bring him from Hel.

But she said, "Þökk will cry with dry eyes over Baldr's journey to the stake. From the older adult's son, neither alive nor dead, never had the advantage. Keep Hel what he has."

It is supposed that Loki, disguised as an older woman, brought the greatest evil among the Æsir. After the death of Baldr, Æsir was very angry with Loki and wanted to capture him. But Loki escaped from Asgard and hid in a mountain. Here, Loki built a house with four doors so that he could look out in all directions. During the day, Loki would often shapeshift into a salmon and hide in the river.

In the evening, Loki sat near the fire pit inside his house and wondered about the punishment of Æsir. While he sat there, he entertained himself by making a fishing net with linen yarn.

One day, Loki was looking out from one of his doors when he saw the Æsir coming to him. He quickly jumped up, threw the linen net into the fire, and then ran down to the river.

When the Æsir arrived at the house, Kvasir was the first one to enter. Kvasir looked around the house and spotted the remains of the net in the fire. He spoke with the Æsir about his findings, and they made a copy of it. All the Æsir began to drag the net and placed it in the waterfall. However, Loki swam in front, moved down, and hid between two stones. The Æsir believed that someone was hiding there, so they threw and pulled out the net. However, he was not there. Again, they threw it.

Loki, realizing he was near the sea, jumped over the net and swam back into the waterfall. This time, the Æsir saw him, and they returned to the waterfall. Thor found himself in the middle of the river and dragged another net toward the sea.

Loki realized that he would have to dive into the sea, though it was dangerous, or jump through the net. He finally decided to throw himself headlong into the net. Thor grabbed the fish. It almost slipped from his hands, but he managed to hold it by the tail. Loki had been captured and could not hope for mercy.

Now that the Æsir had captured Loki, they wanted revenge for the death of Baldr. They dragged Loki to a cave and took three flat stones. They put them on their edges and made a hole through them.

The Æsir caught Loki's sons, Vali and Narfi. They transformed Vali into a wolf that devoured his brother Narfi. Using magic with Narfi's guts, the gods bound Loki, who was then placed on top of the three stones. Skadi took a poisonous snake for the last punishment and placed it near Loki so that its poison dropped to his face. Sigyn, Loki's wife, decided to stay and help Loki by holding a basket on his head to catch the venom of the snake. Every time the bowl is full, she leaves to empty it. At that moment, the poison drips on Loki's face, making him shake violently in pain so that the whole earth trembles.

Chapter 32: Loki's Blood Oath

Loki's parents are Fárbauti and Laufey, and he is a brother of Helblindi and Býleistr. Some people relate to him as a god, while others as a jötunn. There are also those who declare him both. He is a playful being and just as likely to hinder the gods as to help them.

Now, Loki is a jerk. At one party thrown by the god Ægir, Loki became furious at the attendants of Ægir, named Fimafeng and Eldir, for being so helpful and welcoming toward the other gods, whom he saw as being corrupt and shameful of praise. To make his point, Loki killed Fimafeng.

Regardless of the purpose of Loki's jealousy, the gods didn't stand for this act and chased him from the hall. He went into the woods for a time, and the gods went back to their mead.

Upon his return, Loki accosted the outstanding servant, Eldir. Although he dropped Eldir alive, the gods weren't about to invite Loki to join them at the hall. In reply to this, Loki requested the oath sworn by Odin that the two would drink together, and Odin invited the trickster god to the table.

While a god with a little more modesty, or at least a few more considerable tact, might not have attempted to push his luck, Loki started insulting the gods. He insisted that the gods were nervous and sexually diverse. Freyja, being expressly shocked by this, challenged Loki, saying that the latter was forced to be so vitriolic in the appearance of the goddess Frigg, as Frigg knew the destiny and fate of all. Loki snapped back, attacking Freyja for having lain with every god and elf in the hall. The row goes on for quite some time.

The Bifrost Bridge and the World Tree of Yggdrasil in the Underworld

The Bifrost Bridge is mythological in Norse mythology. It crosses the river of Tuoni and connects the Nine Worlds. The Bifrost Bridge is guarded by Heimdallr, whose horn Gjallarhorn gives off a sound that can be heard throughout the nine worlds. It signals the beginning of Ragnarök.

In Norse mythology, Yggdrasil is an immense tree that connects all of the Nine Worlds with its branches and roots. It was believed to be an evergreen ash tree that continued growing as long as it had enough water in its roots.

Yggdrasil, the world tree of Norse mythology, is the giant ash tree that sits in the center of the nine worlds. These nine worlds are

1. Jotunheim (the land of giants)
2. Midgard (the world of men)
3. Asgard (the gods' home)
4. Vanaheim (home of the Vanir gods)
5. Niflheim (home for Norns and frost giants)
6. Muspelheim (home for the fire giants)
7. Helheim (where reside those who died without being buried)
8. Nidavellir (home of the dwarves beneath the earth)
9. Alfheim (home of the elves)

The upper branches of the world tree touch heaven and the Nine Worlds below it, which can be seen from Asgard, where Odin lived. In the Nine Worlds, there are the nine great families of the gods. There are two prominent families: the Aesir and the Vanir. These families are often at war with each other, and that is how things exist in Yggdrasil.

The great ash tree Yggdrasil is sometimes called a "world rune." In Norse mythology, it is a central symbol of existence. It was believed that the well beneath this tree is the source of all wisdom and knowledge. From beyond time, Odin's spirit watches over this well, guarding it for all eternity to keep its secrets safe so that mortals might never discover them.

The Bifrost Bridge is made of two massive slabs of ice that are joined at their bases by a central column. This column is Yggdrasil, whose roots run down through the earth and wind up the bottom of the pillar. Once Yggdrasil has been planted, it will not die until Ragnarok. At that time, the demon-god Loki will be born and cast down from heaven by his brother Thor. Then Yggdrasil will be burned to death with all its roots and branches consumed in flames, taking all of existence with it.

In Gaiman's *The Bridge*, the bridge is not one but two bridges. One, made of ice and forged as a gift from the dwarves to their king in exile, is used only by Odin and his immediate family. The other, with the Bifrost itself bridging them, is used by the gods themselves. Beyond this bridge is an elemental realm where all the elements meet among themselves: fire meets water, air meets earth, and so on. In this realm, Thor has discovered a board that allows him to directly talk to any of them.

Ragnarok or Twilight of the Gods

The gods are not above the power of those higher than them. They, too, must be subject to judgment. They, too, must perish when their allotted time has come. Ragnarok is the name of the twilight of the gods, the period when the end of the gods draws near. The name Ragnarok can be taken to mean the dissolution of the gods or the darkness of the gods. The gods knew that Ragnarok would eventually come. The coming of this time would be foreshadowed by evil warnings, such as increased violence and ill behavior among men.

Ragnarok will be heralded by the crowing of the Aesir cock in Valhalla and the crowing of Hel's cock in the Hell-Ways. Fjalar, the cock of the giants, will also crow, and the hound of Hel will bay far down below Yggdrasil in Niflheim. The world will descend into wickedness for three years, and this will be followed by a long, snowy winter. No warmth will come from the sun, which will be swallowed by the wolf called Skoll. Another wolf will eat the moon. The stars will be extinguished, and earthquakes all around cause the world, even the mountains, to tremble. The Fenris Wolf and Loki will be freed, and the Midgard Serpent will cause the sea's waters to rear up and wash over the land.

Loki will steer a ship made up of the nails of dead men. Rime-Thursar and other giants will follow. All of these wicked creatures—Loki, the Fenris Wolf, the Midgard Serpent, the giant Rym, and Rime-Thursar—will be free to raise their hordes for battle. The Aesir also prepares for war with the sounding of the Gjallarhorn. The gods are roused, and Odin seeks guidance from Mimir's head. The two hosts meet on the field of Vigrid. Odin is first, dressed in his golden armor and brandishing Gungnir, his spear.

Odin and Thor, respectively, prepare to fight the Fenris Wolf and the Midgard Serpent. Thor fought Midgard Serpent and overpowered him, but he only walks nine steps more until he falls dead. The Fenris Wolf swallows Odin until the god is defeated. Other gods among the Aesir die, too. Surtr vanquishes Freyr while Loki and Heimdal slay each other. Surt covers the world in flame, and all things on the earth perish. It sets the stage for a new life. A new land rises, young and green. Plants grow without seeds needing to be sewn. The Sun and her daughter herald a new day. Those Aesir who did not die return, setting the stage for the All-Father, the governor of everything.

Yggdrasil and the Nine Worlds

Yggdrasil is the world tree that connects to nine worlds. The tree roots are in Helheim—a land of death and suffering for those who have wronged. The branches reach into Asgard—a land for those who died fighting bravely or otherwise died with honor. The leaves on the tree are thought to be from Álfheimr—the ground for elves. And at its top, representing the divine world and Odin's home is Valhalla—for all warriors fallen in battle and their families. With the various realms and kingdoms depicted on their branches, this image of the world tree is familiar with modern times.

The tree comprised nine different worlds—one for each of the nine worlds that existed before creating our universe. One story tells that when Ægir, the giant sea deity, was creating Yggdrasil, he made a dwarf help him. The dwarf was named Veðrfölnir, and he took part in crafting every one of Yggdrasil's branches and roots. Veðrfölnir gave each root and branch a name. Some components were named after rivers, seas, mountains, and other geographical features. Some were named after plants and trees. The branches of the tree were named after the world gods who each resided there. In some versions of the story, Ægir had Veðrfölnir carve the names only on one side of each branch to see who would get which character every time it was read backward.

The worlds at Yggdrasil's roots were the following:

1. Helheim—the land for those who died in battle or other violent ways and then went to Hel after death.
2. Asgard—the ground for those who died a glorious death and died with honor (in battle or otherwise).
3. Jötunheimr—the land for those who died a violent death and went to Hel after death.
4. Vogelfjörðr—the ground for those who died in battles with each other or as sacrifices to a greater deity.
5. Niflheim—the land for those who were killed as sacrifices to lesser deities or as sacrifices to their gods.
6. Hvergelmir—the land of immediate punishment and torment of those who die unbaptized.
7. Midgard—the world of humans and elves, created by the gods from the ash produced by Surt's burning (Ragnarök).
8. Muspelheimr—the land for those who died but went to Hel after death.
9. Níðhöggr—the land of those who died in a shipwreck or on a battlefield where they could not be buried properly.

Originally, Yggdrasil's roots were believed to be sunken into Helheim between the Sagas (now called Jötunheimr) and Asgard. However, they are now thought to be growing from a different root than either Helheim or Asgard.

The tree's branches have been interpreted as the worlds among which the Norse believed they traveled. Each of the tree's four root races, or families, had a different color and direction in which they faced. They could be found in these colors on the tree:

- Vanic: white
- Aesir: red
- Asynjur: blue or green
- Rime: black

These groups were said to be from the beginning of time to ensure that all life was provided and protected. The tree's branches were said to be named after these four families.

Chapter 33: Egyptian Mythology

What Is an Egyptian Myth?

Egyptian mythology is the compilation of myths from ancient Egypt, which describe the actions of the Egyptian gods as a part of human history. The beliefs that these myths express are an essential part of ancient Egyptian religion. Mythology can be seen as an attempt to explain the world in terms of personal beings and their actions. These include:

- gods and goddesses
- spirits (namely, a person's ka)
- dead humans

Egyptian mythology is among the oldest national myths of literate civilization. It developed as it had been passed down through oral tradition over thousands of years. The Egyptians believed that only a few generations back, people descended from gods, known as the father gods, who ruled Egypt before it was divided into independent kingdoms. At one point, in all likelihood, during the Third Dynasty of Egypt, a group of ancient Egyptian deities came to be viewed as entirely "Egyptian" and not "fairy-like," like some other deities such as Hathor and Thoth. For example, Isis was first worshiped as the goddess who would give life after death to her devotees.

But over time, she became the goddess of resurrection and life. This view of the deities changed as the Egyptians' ideas changed.

Concept of Afterlife

The Egyptian afterlife was one of the most popular and long-lasting in human history. A systematic cosmology codified about 2,500 years ago made it possible to imagine a life after death.

Egyptians developed extensive rituals and complex funerary customs, including preparing the body, protecting it from decay, maintaining space for it in the tomb with food offerings and spells against intrusion or destruction by enemies or even envoys from other regions of the dead's kingdom. The ancient Egyptians considered that the maintenance of their bodies would pave the way for immortality. For this reason, they mummified corpses between 2181 and 1458 BC.

The ancient Egyptians hoped to enjoy an afterlife that resembled their lives on earth as closely as possible. It was a realm of everlasting existence. The deceased entered the afterlife with all the power and privileges they held in life. Egyptians also believed that a person's life on earth was merely a prelude to their eternal afterlife. They continued to worship gods from their earthly lives, who had powers to assist them in eternity. They also hoped that their worldly actions would have a positive bearing on their eternal fate. There were a few exceptions: traitors and heretics were believed to be eternally damned.

The Egyptians believed in four types of an afterlife:

1. The Afterlife of Annihilation: The deceased is eradicated, along with their physical body (like being wiped out of existence).
2. The Afterlife of Judgment: After death, the deceased is judged by Osiris, god of the underworld. The dead would spend eternity evaluating the souls in his kingdom and helping with his work on earth.
3. The Afterlife of Eternal Reward: The deceased is rewarded with eternal bliss.
4. The Afterlife of Eternal Punishment: The deceased is punished with eternal torment.

In the afterlife, the deceased enters a realm similar to that of existence on earth; however, everything is made out of some imperishable material (gold, precious gemstones, etc.), and to an extent, it resembles a fairytale world. There are no mosquitoes or flies. There are no diseases or pain. Death is simply a state from which one awoke to a more pleasant life. The social relationships between the living and the dead mirror those of the present, except women can be more easily identified as equal to men.

What Is the Concept of an Egyptian God or Goddess?

Egyptian gods and goddesses are just some of the various deities that are part of the ancient Egyptian religion. These entities, who are often the most powerful and most popular in Egyptian mythology, represent distinct aspects of nature and society.

Beyond this basic definition, there's not much more to say about these deities because information about them is scattered at best. The lack of extant records means we know very little about how they play into everyday life or their role in society. However, one thing is sure: Egyptians revered these entities as a fundamental part of their culture for thousands of years before Christianity assimilated Egypt.

But the question remains: How can we define an Egyptian god in terms that apply to this modern, rational world? It's a difficult question to answer, but here is my best attempt at answering it.

An Egyptian god is an entity that is worshipped as a fundamental part of civilization. The concept of a specific god or goddess would permeate every aspect of society. All facets of culture would be carried out according to the wishes of these deities. Human beings are born into a system where certain gods will play more significant roles than others, and these individuals will possess greater power than their human peers.

In the ancient Egyptian world, these gods are supposedly responsible for creating the universe. They govern the globe daily, and they are revered as living entities that could intervene in human affairs.

It was a fundamental concept to ancient Egyptians because it dictates how they live their life. If there were greater forces that controlled all aspects of existence, it was essential to do things that pleased them. For example, the Nile River would flood each year; if it did so without fail and within a predictable cyclical pattern, this was because of Ma'at, a goddess who personified justice and order. The ancient Egyptians were easily able to envision the world as being in equilibrium, and they loved to make comparisons between Ma'at and other areas of their lives. They believed that this cosmic order took care of their every whim.

During the New Kingdom, Egypt experienced a time of relative peace and prosperity under the rule of Pharaoh Tutankhamun. The pharaoh encouraged this order and harmony by commissioning poets that spoke of Ma'at in poetic terms. This was a way to tell everyone how they should behave. The Egyptians were also able to understand how cosmic forces affected them on a daily basis by means of their calendar, which was based on lunar cycles. The calendar and the months were organized by the rising of the star Sirius, which was directly related to Ma'at. The stars never moved from their places so that there would always be fifteen days of both Thoth and Nut on each side of Sirius. The lunar calendar laid down a base for the Egyptian timekeeping system.

The Egyptians emulated many natural phenomena to make their lives more pleasant through Ma'at. They believed that life was all about balance and that everything had its proper place in the universe, including human beings. Egyptians wanted to have a sense of peace that was not related to the natural world. They used poetry and other literature as their way to emulate order. They also set up gods, goddesses, and other powerful spirits so that they could live under them and follow Ma'at. By doing this, Egyptians thought they were accepting fate for what it was and living in harmony with their surroundings.

The Egyptians did not only pattern their way of living after the natural world. They also tried to mimic the actions of their deities. For example, by creating sculptures and drawings that illustrated a god or goddess engaged in some kind of activity, they were able to follow this model.

There are many stories from the New Kingdom about people who were punished for breaking Ma'at in some way. When one broke the law or was disrespectful toward other gods, they would fall ill and die without being able to understand what happened to them.

Chapter 34: How Was Ancient Egypt Ruled?

Egypt was ruled by a pharaoh, who, with a few exceptions, were all male. He would have been the oldest son of the last pharaoh. When you use written records to find out what life was like for Egyptians, you often find that some are pretty poor and poorly treated. But there are also stories about noblewomen who could inherit property or become rulers in their own right if they had no brothers to take over from their father when he retired.

In ancient Egypt, an elaborate social hierarchy placed people in different classes based on where they lived and their jobs. At the top of this system was the king. He had absolute authority over everyone in ancient Egypt. The king was the highest living god, and many people believed that he could make decisions directly with the gods without having to consult any others.

Below him were nobles with titles such as priest, overseer, or vizier. These were men who did not have to work for a living, and they were responsible for managing the country on behalf of the king. Beneath them were members of two kinds of middle classes: administrators and craftsmen. The administrators ran the government offices, and the craftsmen made goods for sale in shops. The only way to become a member of these middle classes was to be born into them. They were closed groups that controlled their members to make it challenging for people from other backgrounds to become part of them.

At the bottom of this society were peasants or farmers, who were mainly responsible for raising crops and livestock on land owned by nobles. There was also a middle class of workers such as fishermen, butchers, and bakers who did not own land. Below them were people with jobs considered dirty, such as butchers, tanners, and metalworkers, many of whom had to work in their own homes. The people at the bottom, along with slaves, made up the majority of the population.

The lower classes lived in small villages and towns where they were under the complete control of their noble masters. Workers who lived in villages like this were called peasants. The peasants had to pay tribute to their aristocratic landlords, and so they often ended up being forced to sell part of their crops to buy food for their families.

Pharaohs ruled Egypt for most of its history. They also controlled the lower classes, but sometimes other government members, such as priests or viziers, were involved in leading and holding critical religious offices.

Egyptian mythology presents a complex and diverse set of beliefs about the gods. The ancient Egyptian language had no word for religion, so the ancient Egyptians viewed their gods as part of everyday life.

Horus

Ancient Egyptians worshiped many gods, but Horus might have been the most popular one. He was a sky god with the head of a falcon or a man and a human body. The pharaohs identified themselves as Horus on earth, and he became associated with kingship. He also had close ties to life and fertility in some versions of his legend.

Horus was the son of Osiris and Isis. When Horus grew up, he became a great warrior who defeated Set in a battle. Because of this, Horus became associated with war and conflict. He carried a shield that represented the protection of the people and a curved sword that brought justice to the land. His right eye represented the sun, which had an important role in Egyptian mythology as it gave light to the world.

As the sky god, Horus was associated with some other gods. He was sometimes linked with the sun god Ra, and as a child, he was connected with Re, the Egyptian creator god. He was also associated with Hathor and Bastet.

Osiris

Osiris, in Egyptian mythology, is the god of the afterlife and the resurrected. He was believed to judge people after death then present their souls to the gods for either approval or destruction. Osiris was usually depicted as green-skinned with white hair and a beard, wearing a crown consisting of ostrich feathers on top and a set of red Andes stones around it.

He was born with his sister Isis, who had at first difficult labor, but as she could not give birth due to her beauty, she was advised by her brother to bathe in the Nile. She did so and cleansed herself; when she returned to her husband, she gave birth with speed and power surpassing that of the gods. It is said that afterward, he accomplished every form of magic. He spoke the truth and never violated his word, and as long as he lived, no one dared tell lies. He met his destruction at the hands of the evil god Set to whom he had given his sister Isis to wife. He was killed by being entombed in wood and dragged along.

Anubis

Anubis is the god of the afterlife in Egyptian mythology. He served as a guide to souls and one of the judges of the dead. As a god, he was connected with mummification and burial rites and watched over blacksmiths, embalmers, and others whose jobs meant contact with corpses.

He was often said to be clothed in bandages that hid his proper form (except for his black-painted face), but he could appear animal-headed when defending Egypt or transporting souls to the underworld. The Egyptian black jackal can be seen as an early symbolic ursine manifestation of this jackal god.

Anubis was the god who helped Isis locate Osiris' body and embalmed him for internment. Like his father, Osiris, who he took over for as ruler of the dead, Anubis took on many of the traits of Ra, including his solar disk with Uraeus. He also was depicted as holding a staff entwined with serpents, just as Ra did.

Isis

Isis, originally a goddess in ancient Egyptian religion, was later worshipped as an aspect of Hathor. She was typically depicted as the mother of Horus, and she acted as his advocate. Isis also wore a vulture crown with the double crown of Upper and Lower Egypt on top. The Book of the Dead states that Isis wore a unique collar around her neck with two large pearls on it while other deities had one.

Isis is the most popular goddess in Egyptian mythology. Her worship was widespread in ancient Egypt and led to an abundance of her many myths and legends. It is even suggested that a specific form of magic was based upon this worship. Isis was usually portrayed as a mother figure with her hands resting on or hugging Horus, an infant god born through her womb. She is described as being motherly and nurturing, which shows how important she was to the followers of ancient Egypt. Isis' titles include Mistress, Lady, and "She Who Was Pleased."

Isis was unique in many ways to ancient Egyptians. She was a goddess of fertility, so it was not unusual for her to be depicted as having an infant on her lap. She is said to have a cobra upon her headdress and a vulture crown with two large pearls on top; this showed that she was aligned with the Upper Egyptian gods and goddesses, who wore the Double Crown that depicted a vulture holding the sun disk. Isis is said to only wear one crown in contrast with others of her role, which shows how different and unusual she truly is.

Isis also has many titles, which are all concerned with fertility issues. She was known as Mistress of the Southern Sky, Mistress of the Seasons, and Mistress of the Morning.

Ra

Ra was the most prominent god in ancient Egyptian mythology. He is usually painted either as a hawk or as a man with the head of a hawk. He was associated with crowing (like the sun), and he helped keep time during its daily cycle. He also protected people from illness or disasters, so people would pray to him when they needed protection. In addition to being seen as an all-powerful god who needed little help from other gods, Ra was viewed as the son of Atum and Kheprera (creators) and father to Shu and Tefnut (goddesses).

Ra was one of the first gods to be worshiped in ancient Egypt, and he rose to become one of the most important. His leading role was that of the sun god. In addition to being a symbol of light, Ra was also seen as a creator god who brought all things into existence. Ra thus represented creation and destruction. In artistic depictions, Ra is usually shown with a long falcon's head and an arrow that points downward at the mouth; this symbolizes his power over air and fire (the word *ra* actually means "fire"). He also carries an ankh, the Egyptian symbol of life.

Although Ra was often said to have created himself, he was also said to have been created by Atum (god of creation). Atum was a sun god who self-created at the beginning of time and made all other gods. He is usually portrayed in art as a man with the head of a beetle, and this symbolizes how he came into existence from nothingness. Ra's son, Shu (god of air), is thus said to be the product of Atum's tears, which were shed when he was lonely. It is because Shu was born from these tears that he became associated with moisture and humidity.

Thoth

Thoth is the god of wisdom and writing. Sometimes he was depicted as a man, and other times he appeared as a baboon. Thoth was considered one of the most powerful gods of ancient Egypt, credited with creating language and measuring time! As a result, many humans would go to him for help with writing letters or legal documents. He even helped judge when people died and were sent to heaven or hell (though not all Egyptians agreed that this should be his responsibility).

Thoth is often pictured with an ostrich feather headdress, which was a symbol of royalty. A baboon was typically thought of as a servant or herald, so Thoth's association with this domesticated animal makes his close association with majesty in this aspect seem appropriate.

Thoth has been interpreted as being the brother of the Greek god Hermes, and sometimes you might see Thoth and Hermes together in paintings. He also shares symbols and "magic" methods with both Isis (the mother goddess) and Osiris (the god of death).

Chapter 35: Ra's Journey to the Underworld

Ra is one of the most popular gods in ancient Egypt. He had many duties on earth, but his most crucial task was overseeing the sun's daily movement across the sky. When he became older and weaker, Ra decided that he would like to pass on his responsibilities to someone else before he died. It was unthinkable for any god in ancient times that another god would be expected to take their place if they died.

As Ra went through puberty, his journey led him to some of his most powerful enemies, as well as some of his closest allies. Along the way, he gained a new understanding and respect for his powers and abilities. He went through many challenges that he had never had to face before, such as climbing a mountain of sand dunes on the back of a crocodile and transforming into all kinds of people and animals to spy on others to find out their weaknesses. He even transformed into other gods to practice their abilities until he became proficient and was no longer exhausted from using them.

He gained the ability to change his age and even his size to not be worn out from holding heavy loads for long periods. It had helped him in his journey by allowing him to get further and faster than he would have been able to on foot.

Ra's journey was full of action, humor, and adventure. Along the way, he met many other gods and some humans. The humorous scenes are very entertaining, while the action scenes are fascinating. Ra's journey took him down a path that only led him back up into the light once he had completed his task. Ra's trip to the underworld shows you an example of how a god deals with the struggles of growing up through a series of exciting and humorous tales.

According to the ancient Egyptians, Ra is the creator or originator of all forms of life. He called all creatures into existence by their secret names. Humans were created from his tears and sweat, and he traveled the world on two boats. His mythical eye said that, in the beginning, Ra saw everything to be in perfection, which brought him to tears, which, as the legend continues, became humans. When Ra realized that humans were plotting against him, he decided to punish them. He summoned his divine eye, also referred to as the goddess Hathor. Hathor was transformed into a lioness called Sekhmet and caused massive bloodshed. Before Sekhmet could consume all human beings because he had become bloodthirsty, the god Ra got her drunk with beer, and the killings stopped.

When Isis desired to learn Ra's secret name, the goddess used clay and spit and drooled on Ra's chin, and Isis ended up creating a poisonous snake. Ra was bitten by the snake and asked the gods to help him recover from the pain. Isis offered to help but only if Ra gave her the secret to his powers.

Ra, the supreme sun god, was believed to traverse the sky every day on a solar boat and pass through the underworld (Duat) every night to another ship, only to reappear in the east every morning. The Alet was the boat god Ra used to move from sunlight to noon, and the Seklet boat was used from noon to sunset. During the journey, Ra had always been fighting many battles against Apep, the serpent god, the master of evil or darkness.

The course of the boats was determined by the goddess Ma'at. Thoth and Ma'at stood on either side of the ship while Horus was the one who steered. Two fish—Abtu and Ant—swam in front of the boat to ensure that the journey was successful. At night, the god Upuaut was at the prow to help steer the ship. One way of knowing when Apep was successful was when a storm would ensue. A solar eclipse happened when Apep was swallowed by the boat. Early Egyptians learned how to defeat Apep by reciting verses in the temple of Amon-Ra in Thebes.

Egyptians believed that, on the two boats, Ra carried the prayers and blessings of the living and those of the souls of the dead. He was thought to carry out this daily duty along with the other deities who helped him. He was always traveling with Seth and Mehen. In his journeys, the god Ra changed his form from Atum, as the Mesektet boat prepared him for his rebirth every morning.

Ra was the ruler of the sky and the earth, and she was the first being and the father of Shu and Tefnut and the grandfather of Geb and Nut. The children, Osiris, Isis, Seth, and Nephthys, owe their existence to the god Ra. It was believed that Ra emerged from the ocean as the first rays from the sea made their way to heaven. Shu and Tefnut emerged from this phenomenon via the seed of his loins.

Ancient Egyptians used to bury a solar boat whenever a pharaoh died; they believed that the ruler needed transportation in the afterlife. The boat was also referred to as the boat of the millions because of all the gods and souls needed as a crew to fight evil during its journey.

The god Ra was always alone during the day. At night, he was accompanied by other gods for protection. On other occasions, he is described as wearing a large sun disk on the head, while, in the underworld, Ra had a ram head. Ra is often depicted as the creator, and he is also the god of life.

The age of the sun god is considered to be 1,000 years. Ra's birthday has been celebrated on March 28 each year since 500 BC.

The son of Ra was Horus. The pair are shown together on many different objects as the guardians of a good harvest and the defeat of evil. They were also the protectors of all dead souls, which include deceased kings and priests. In one scene, Horus and Isis are depicted as protecting the three-headed god Sobek.

In ancient Egypt, there were many deities that represented various aspects of life and death; Ra was at the top of this hierarchy, among them being a protector against evil forces, such as destruction and disease.

Chapter 36: The Book of the Dead and the Path of Osiris

The Egyptians told us that we are born from death and when we die, our hearts weigh our deeds, but they also left us a map of the afterlife. Understanding Egyptian mythology can help us better understand ourselves and triumph over fear, anxiety, and depression. Let's discuss this topic in more detail.

In death, the ancient Egyptians believed they needed to be re-animated by Osiris before entering the afterlife. Osiris is the god of rebirth and regeneration (Egyptian God). The Book of the Dead is their story of how these rituals were performed. The Egyptians believed that after death, the soul faced many challenges. The deceased had to negotiate countless obstacles and hazards, including fiends and demons sent by the god of chaos Ammit, to reach the paradise of Aaru (Egyptian heaven).

The book describes all functions in life and how they're transferred into death. It includes the following:

- *To be reborn into Osiris' kingdom:* The deceased had to demonstrate that he or she led a virtuous life. The heart was measured toward the feather of truth to test a person's moral purity. If they failed, their soul was devoured by Ammit in their heart. If they passed, their soul would travel to Osiris' kingdom.

- *To be resurrected in the afterlife:* The Egyptians believed that one had to be complete, which meant having the correct body parts. The Egyptians practiced mummification so their bodies could endure forever. A person's organs were buried beneath their feet, and enough food was placed with them to support them in the afterlife. Deceased men wore a kilt around their waist called a kalasiris. Dead women wore a dress called a sheath dress.

The Egyptians believed that they would need to take on different roles in the afterlife. A person's role in life is reflected in how they are buried, as well as the amulets and artifacts buried with them. In their afterlife, women were given men's clothes, and men were given women's clothes to wear. These changes are documented by their tomb paintings and their bodies being preserved accordingly (Egyptian mummies).

The Book of the Dead is often depicted with the deceased receiving spells or being judged in front of Osiris. It was meant to assist a person in navigating through the afterlife. The ancient Egyptians had their gods intercede on their behalf, provide spells that would protect them, and give them instructions on overcoming the threats they would face in the afterlife.

The ancient Egyptians considered that the deceased could live forever in conjunction with Osiris, god of vegetation and fertility. The Book of the Dead is a way to guide people into Osiris' kingdom. The deceased would be assigned a role in this kingdom based upon how they lived their lives. They would be rewarded or punished accordingly.

To be judged, the deceased face the gods and goddesses of the underworld. The Egyptians believed that each god was personified by an animal or a physical object, as well as a divine force that determined that person's fate. According to the Book of the Dead, the same animals were also used to protect the deceased.

The ancient Egyptians thought that a soul was only allowed to enter Aaru (Egyptian heaven) after Osiris had transformed it. This transformation is referred to as "the resolution of the soul." The ancient Egyptians believed that the resolution of the soul had four different aspects.

In the underworld, the deceased became a judge for other souls. Some of these were not as fortunate as the deceased, and Ammit, the devourer of souls, would eat them. If they escaped her clutches, they would be eaten by a demon named "the eater of the dead."

The Book of the Dead is a compilation of funerary texts used in ancient Egypt. The ancient Egyptians referred to their journey through the afterlife as "the making perfect" or "the becoming divine." Only one copy of each book has been found, leading scholars to believe that an individual commissioned each book. Each book is unique due to its customized inscriptions.

The ancient Egyptians believed that the deceased would be assigned a role in this kingdom based upon how they lived their lives. They would be rewarded or punished accordingly. In the underworld, the deceased became a judge for other souls. Some of these were not as fortunate as the deceased, and Ammit, the devourer of souls, would eat them. If they escaped her clutches, they would be eaten by a demon named "the eater of the dead."

Books of the Dead belonging to wealthy deceased were often illustrated with a vignette at the beginning and a scene depicting their judgment in the afterlife. Other books were mere collections of incantations, while others contained rituals to protect the dead or guide them through the underworld. In addition to being protected from these dangers, it was also thought that one's afterlife would be more pleasant if the spells in the Book of the Dead were performed correctly.

As in life, these texts served to protect the dead against their enemies and guide them through the dangers of the underworld. All of these were conceptually written for a single individual, meant to be used by those buried in a particular tomb. They were not "published" in a modern sense but rather circulated among Egyptians who possibly had copies at different stages of their lives.

Book of the Dead refers to some ancient Egyptian funerary papyri containing spells intended to help one reach the afterlife safely. The spells were originally written on papyrus scrolls but later became inscribed on tomb walls and coffins. The Book of the Dead was usually compiled in funerary amulets for the deceased to keep close at hand. The Book of the Dead is a compilation of these various texts and their accompanying illustrations. It is not a religious text as such and has no direct connection to any worshiping of the Egyptian gods. The text is made up of a number of individual spells that are the references for mummification and burial rituals.

When one follows the path to the afterlife, they must make many stops along the way. The first stop is the Hall of Truth. Here, those who have not earned their title of "devoted servant" (a title that is closely related to the Book of the Dead) are judged. The Hall of Truth has many hallways and rooms that do not seem to have any connection. It contains many obstacles that must be overcome to move forward.

Chapter 37: The List of Black Lands and Gates in the Underworld

According to the Amduat, the Tuat is divided into twelve regions, with each part representing one of the twelve hours of the night. Each area has its geographical features and is inhabited by its own set of deities, some of whom temporarily join Ra's crew to get his barge from one end of the region to the other. One such god called the Lady of the Boat aboard only through a particular area. Her duty is to protect Ra and his barge while it is in her territory. In addition to deities and various physical features, some regions also have hazards that need to be negotiated. The solar barge itself changes depending on where it happens to be at the moment. For example, the mummified Ra is usually seated either in an open space in the middle of the boat or under a kind of tent. Still, at one point, a friendly giant serpent comes aboard and forms a new tent with its body to protect Ra on that part of his journey.

Below are highly abbreviated descriptions of the twelve regions according to the Amduat.

1. In one illustration for this region, the sun god stands in the middle of the barge in his ba form, a ram-headed

man with a solar disk between his horns. In another, he is shown as a scarab beetle. Egyptologist Erik Hornung states that this is intended to show that the sun's journey is expected to be completed successfully. Nine baboons in this region have the job of opening the gates of the Tuat so that the solar barge can go through, while another nine sings to Ra. Because the sun is dead and has no light at this point, there are magical serpents who provide light in this region. Various other deities praise the sun god, who asks permission to enter the Tuat proper. Permission is granted, and the baboons open the doors.

2. Still in his ram-headed form (which with one exception he will keep until the end of the journey), the sun god rides in his barge along a stream. Several rowers propel the barge. Isis and Nephthys are aboard in the form of serpents. Several other barges accompany Ra's boat at this stage. One is the barge of the moon. Another is the barge of Hathor. A god in a lizard form occupies the third barge. The last is the boat of Neper, the god of grain, who is an avatar of Osiris. Many other gods and goddesses are in this region. They praise Ra and ask him to renew himself. Ra replies with blessings for the residents of the area and commands that evil beings be

banished. He then asks for help in his journey across the Tuat.

3. The barge is rowed along with ram-headed Ra in the middle. As in the second region, there are four other boats on the river with the solar barge. The first is called "the boat that capsizes," and it carries Horus deities. The second and third boats are called "the boat of rest" and "the boat of the branch," respectively. Each carries a mummified Osiris. In addition to the main deity, each of these subsidiary boats has a crew of other gods and goddesses. Mummified forms of Osiris appear elsewhere in the illustrations for this region as well.

4. In the fourth region, water does not flow. The barge instead has to be towed over sand, and it is a different barge from the one in the first three regions, having serpents' heads at the prow and stern. The fourth region is called the region of Sokar. Sokar (or Seker) was the Memphite god of the dead. Snakes slither over the sand here, and instead of moving straight across the page, the solar boat now takes a downward path, which goes from the upper right corner to the lower left. One part of the illustration shows two gods guarding the Eye of Ra. These gods are Thoth and Horus. The winged sun disk appears in this region as well, as does the goddess Maat.

5. Still in the region of Sokar, Ra's boat continues its descent, this time moving diagonally downward from the upper left corner to the lower right. The burial mound of Osiris is here, watched over by Isis and Nephthys, who are in bird form as kites. Ra makes various addresses to the beings who live in this region, asking that he be allowed to pass through unmolested.

6. Ra switches to a barge that floats on the water and is paddled by a crewman. Erik Hornung states that this water is the water of Nun. There are four sets of mummified beings, and each set represents the kings of a different cardinal direction. The dead body of Ra is represented by a recumbent man holding the scarab of Khepera over his head, encircled by an enormous serpent. According to Hornung, in this region, the dead body of the sun is conceptualized as the dead body of Osiris, which is reunited with its ba, represented by the scarab.

7. The seventh region is called the Hall of Osiris. Ra is once again depicted as a ram-headed man with a solar disk between his horns. Instead of the usual canopy, he is now covered by an arch made by the giant serpent Mehen. Mehen will continue to protect Ra in this way until Ra is reborn as Khepera and rises as the new sun. Isis stands in the prow with her arms outstretched, using

her magic to make the boat move. The giant serpent Apophis is shown having been defeated. His body is pierced by six knives, while a goddess strangles him near his head, and a god ties up his tail. Horus also appears in this region in the form of a seated man with a hawk's head, on which is the solar disk to which a uraeus is attached. It is Horus's job to make the stars rise and to see to it that time continues to flow. Twelve gods represent the stars, while twelve goddesses represent the hours of the day and night.

8. In this region, Mehen's power gives the crew towing the barge the ability to make progress across the waters. There are four rams depicted here, each with a different headdress. The rams represent manifestations of Tatanen, the god of the primordial mound from which creation arose. Several other deities are depicted, along with looms and other things needed to weave cloth. Of these representations of weaving, Erik Hornung observes that "this theme of this hour is thus the supplying of clothes, which from early times on represented a high priority among the things wished for in the afterlife."

9. One part of the illustrations for this region shows the twelve gods who row Ra's barge. The other job these gods have is to use their paddles to splash water onto the

riverbank to use the spirits who dwell there. Ra also promises to provide food and drink for the beings who live in this region. Besides the barge crew, twelve goddesses sing praises to Osiris and twelve fire-breathing uraei who use their power to protect Ra as he passes by.

10. Ra continues to stand under the arch of Mehen's body, but now he carries an ankh in his right hand, while his left holds a staff in the shape of a serpent. A series of illustrations show four gods holding spears, four holding arrows, and four holding bows. Ra bids these gods destroy his enemies with their weapons. The spirits of those who have drowned dwell in the waters here; Ra promises that they can enter paradise even though they haven't been mummified. It is in the tenth region that Ra and Khepera are joined together in preparation for sunrise. It is represented in part by an illustration of a scarab beetle pushing an elliptical shape representing the horizon. In his baboon manifestation, Thoth holds the Eye of Horus to be healed by the goddess Sekhmet.

11. The text for this region states that the deities who live here are guiding the sun to the eastern horizon so that he can rise again. Ra rides in his boat covered by Mehen, but elsewhere in this part, Mehen appears as an enormously long snake being carried along by twelve gods who go on foot. Their job is to see to it that Mehen also arrives

safely at the eastern horizon. A fourfold manifestation of the goddess Neith is found here, as are a series of pits of fire in which the enemies of Ra are consumed. Each hole has its attendant deity tending the flames.

12. After a long and dangerous journey, Ra's solar barge finally arrives at the eastern horizon. Ram-headed Ra stands in the middle of the boat under his Mehen-canopy, while Khepera occupies the prow in the form of a scarab. One portion of the text in Budge's translation reads: "Then this exceptional god taketh up his post in the Eastern Horizon of heaven, and Shu receiveth him, and his cometh into being in the East." But before sunrise can happen, Ra's barge has to travel the length of a giant serpent named Ankhneteru. For this part of the journey, the barge is towed by twelve gods and twelve goddesses. The goddesses towing the barge also have the duty of creating breezes on earth. Twelve additional goddesses carry fire-breathing serpents on their shoulders. The serpents use their fire to repel the enemies of Ra, especially the demon serpent Apophis. Another twelve gods sing praises to Ra. The final illustration shows a curved wall at the rightmost edge of the papyrus. It represents the horizon. The god Khepera, in the form of a scarab beetle, pushes the sun disk through the middle of the wall. The disk is placed

beneath the head of the air god Shu, whose arms extend along the inner perimeter of the wall. At the bottom of the wall is a mummy representing Ra's night body, which he has cast off and which will be destroyed now that he has been born again as the rising sun.

Chapter 38: Seto Mamiut: God of Chaos, Magic, and Animals

Seto Mamiut is an ancient Egyptian deity who's been given credit for creating chaos and magic. He was often considered to be in cahoots with Set, but it's not clear the extent of his involvement. In addition to being a god of chaos, magic, and animals, Seto Mamiut is also associated with fertility. The god presides over the cycle of seasons and can be identified as a wind god who renews life during periods when little or no rain falls.

It is believed that he can also curse people through animal noises like crowing roosters or roaring lions. He is said to be able to change men into animals and vice versa. He is worshiped when Egypt experiences chaos and disorder.

Although not very much is known about Seto Mamiut, the fact that he has many different roles makes it difficult for people to determine whether he should be worshipped widely, especially as the preference seems to change with each dynasty. As a result, monuments dedicated to Seto Mamiut are scarce and are primarily found in Lower Egypt.

Also, there is little information about his iconography since he's often confused with Set or Sobek. The most persistent image of him is that of him holding a flaming torch. He's also portrayed with a cobra on his head and body covered in lotus flowers. The image differs depending on which period it was created, and some pictures of him are more straightforward than others, which could be attributed to his various roles.

Seto Mamiut is also depicted as a man dressed in green robes holding a flaming torch with two snakes wrapped around it while standing atop crocodiles. He also often wears a crown of lotus flowers. To identify themselves as followers of Seto Mamiut, the Egyptians depicted him with an upside-down jasper udjat (eye of Horus) amulet.

The first references to Seto Mamiut were discovered in the pyramid texts, dating back to the Old Kingdom. The texts portrayed him as a powerful god who could bring about chaos through magic. As time progressed, Seto Mamiut became more involved with creation and fertility through the illustrations in tombs and temples from various periods; however, there wasn't much consistency in how he was portrayed. As a result, he became associated with other deities such as Hathor, who would occasionally be depicted with him.

There are many references to Seto Mamiut in the Book of the Dead, written during the New Kingdom period of

Egyptian history when Seto Mamiut started to decline in popularity. Through these references, Seto Mamiut has been praised for his powers and skills and his ability to bring about harmony and fertility. In some part, he's asked not to weave spells that would cause poverty or sickness but instead work toward bringing about peace and plenty.

In some parts of the Book of the Dead, Seto Mamiut is referred to as a god who could destroy "the world in one instant" through his magic. In contrast, another part of the book would refer to Seto Mamiut as a god that could "cause the dead to walk." It's not clear what perspective was more popular through time, but it's possible that these references were contradictory and that both ideas were considered equally important.

This confusion in iconography ultimately led to more people worshipping him because he was multifaceted. He wasn't just a devious magician or an upside-down Anubis but also a god who brought about fertility and stability to Egypt.

The ancient Egyptians would sometimes associate Seto Mamiut with Sobek, which ultimately led to his decline. Sobek was frequently worshiped for various reasons; he was associated with Seto Mamiut in a few images where both deities were shown together. As a result, the religious movement of honoring Sobek more heavily instead of Seto Mamiut caused the god to become obscure. It was eventually proposed that Seto Mamiut be incorporated into Anubis' cult because of their multiple overlapping roles, which created further confusion and ultimately led to his downfall as a popular deity.

Another hypothesis is that Seto Mamiut started to decline in popularity after being associated with Anubis in some images. It could have been because there was never a single depiction of Seto Mamiut without Anubis, which is a bit confusing since they seem to be separate deities. There are also references to Seto Mamiut within tombs and temples from various periods, making it unclear whether one particular deity or multiple deities are worshiped.

Seto Mamiut had several different origins and associations, making it difficult for people to determine his role in Egyptian mythology. The Egyptians initially associated him with the moon and crocodile, so he was depicted as a man dressed in green robes with snakes wrapped around his head and holding a flaming torch.

As time passed, Seto Mamiut became more associated with other elements of creation such as fertility, creating chaos, agriculture, animals, and humans. People eventually began to confuse Seto Mamiut with Anubis in artwork, depicting him as the god of magic or the left eye of Horus. This confused identification led to Seto Mamiut being worshipped for different purposes than originally intended by Egyptians.

Even though the Egyptian god Seto Mamiut was neglected and forgotten during this period, he continued to take part in the mythology of the Egyptians. He would often be referenced within spells and prayers but never fully incorporated into the pantheon. His role as husband to Isis was later given to Horus, who became identified as Isis' husband. Also, Seto Mamiut was associated with Hathor in some images.

Some historians believe that Seto Mamiut's cult continued to exist through time by being incorporated into a local cult in Nubia known as the Red-Headed or Termit. These beliefs continued into the Christian era. One reason for this is that Seto Mamiut was depicted with a crescent moon and a crown of flail on his head, similar to how Christian art showed Jesus Christ.

Like many other Egyptian gods, Seto Mamiut had temples built in his honor throughout time by Egyptians. These temples were typically constructed with pyramids or obelisks due to the god's link to creation and fertility. For example, one temple was built in Abydos during the Roman period of history because Seto Mamiut was associated with Osiris.

Another temple built for Seto Mamiut was constructed in the fifteenth century at a religious site for Islamic worship. This temple was located on the Hill of Gebel Silsila, currently situated in Upper Egypt near Aswan. Many inscriptions have been found in this area that link to Seto Mamiut, such as the Lake of Seti. His name has been replaced with another Egyptian god named Set or Seth.

So far, no cult center has been found for this god except at Lisht. The god was considered essential at Lisht, where he was mainly linked to the cult of Osiris. Seto Mamiut played a role in the resurrection of Osiris and the creation legend. The god is recognized as a divine speaker who proclaims his will and reveals the secrets of all things to various gods. Seto Mamiut is also known for his ability to repel snakes and scorpions from multiple temples dedicated to him.

Chapter 39: Amset, Hapy, Duamutef, Qebehsenuef, and Kebebasuf in the Underworld

In the ancient Egyptian religion, the underworld is where the soul would go after death to be judged and decide its place in the afterlife. It is also a place that many gods live, and they have important roles to play. The underworld is governed by Osiris, king of the dead.

This chapter will explore some of these gods in detail—their appearance, function, connection to other deities—and provide a glimpse into what it might have been like for an ancient Egyptian not just after death but also during various stages in life before it.

First, we have Amset, Hapy, Duamutef, Qebehsenuef, and Kebebasuf in the underworld. They are the four sons of Horus (also called Imsety, Hapy, Duamutef, and Qebehsenuef). They act as a guard of the canopic jars in which the internal organs of the deceased were stored. Sometimes they are depicted as a single four-headed being named Imiut or Imyuty. Each son protected one organ:

- Amset: stomach
- Hapy: lungs
- Duamutef: liver

- Qebehsenuef: intestines/colon

The four sons of Horus were supposedly created by the god Thoth, known as Imhotep, in earlier times. But before they were actual gods, they were considered the four gods that represented different aspects of man:

- Amset: the countenance
- Hapy: the eye
- Duamutef: the phallus
- Qebehsenuf: the head

Amset is the eldest son of Horus. He is portrayed with a human head and a jackal's head connected by an elongated neck so that he also has the protective properties of both gods in one being. Amset's protection is of the stomach and the bowels. He is known to be a loyal protector and defender of the inhabitants of the Duat, another name for the underworld, which is believed to be similar to what we call today limbo or purgatory.

Hapy is represented as a mummified body with an elongated neck and arms that reached down to his feet. He has a human trunk with an ape's head at one end but with a falcon's head at the other end. It is because Hapy protects the lungs and is the breath of life. He is also known as a fertility god since he brings rainfall and blocks the sun from drying up plants; thus, they grow more abundantly.

Duamutef is depicted as a mummy with a jackal's head, and his protection is of the liver. He is seen as a defender of the sun god and the pharaoh.

Qebehsenuef has a human head with the distinctive falcon's head. He represents the head, in general, and guards the intestines or colon. Qebehsenuef protects Ra, known as Harmachis or "Horus in the horizon," which symbolizes sunrise.

There are various associations between the four sons and the gods of air. Amset is pictured as carrying a sun disk, and it is said that he was born as the son of Re. Amset protects against snakebites and against all dangers that come through water or the air. However, he cannot harm snakes and scorpions nor anything that belonged to his father, Osiris, who is considered vulnerable in this way.

As for Hapy, he is pictured carrying the papyrus plant, which is often associated with air and breath and fertility since it is used to make bandages and absorbent pads for menstruation as tampons. Because Hapi is the Nile god, who brings fertility to Egypt through water, he becomes intimately involved with the preparation of corpses by embalmers, who are also inundated in fluids during their messy work.

There are also links between the four sons and the four cardinal points of the universe, although it is unclear whether the sons are supposed to protect everything from one direction or whether they just tend to certain things.

As for Duamutef, he is associated with the north, as I mentioned above, protecting against snakebites. As for Hapy, he is also associated with the north since he brings water to Egypt from that direction during flooding seasons. He is only happy when inundated by water and when embalmers are immersed in fluids while working on corpses, so it seems as though this is a functional association and not just a geographic one.

As for Amset, he is associated with either the east or west as the protector of the Duat. Qebehsenuef is connected to the south since he resides in the underworld and has a sun protection function.

The four sons are mainly considered to be protectors against evil from any direction, and they are involved with life, death, and rebirth. They are associated intimately with embalming since this is seen as a transformative process involving protection and regeneration.

In their role of defending against evil, they guard coffins during internment and protect people against certain dangers in life after death, such as snakes, scorpions, insects, and even fire.

When a body dies, the soul is led by Anubis into the afterlife, but he has to pass through many dangers and obstacles. The four sons protect the deceased through these dangerous tests and guard him in his tomb while he sleeps. Thus, they are known as "sons of Horus," although this name evolved from an earlier one that means "protectors of Horus."

The four sons of Horus are also thought to mediate between humans and other deities. They brought food to their father when he was reborn on earth during summertime after his winter death in the underworld. They offer food to the dead, and they are sometimes thought to sleep with Osiris in the underworld, thus protecting him against evil. They also protect the deceased from "dismemberment" by Osiris' enemies who want to steal his organs. After the people of Egypt began practicing mummification, there was a meaningful connection between this depiction of embalming and healing with regeneration.

Having all four protective functions for human life makes it possible for them to become very active within the other myths about how kingship comes into existence in Egypt. The King of Egypt, who also represents Horus, was the center of Egyptian religious and political life. Four aspects of Horus were blended into one general concept of kingship: the god as king, son of Re, priest of Re, and preserver and protector.

The four sons may be associated with the four cardinal directions because they serve as protectors for a person going through life. And there is probably also some influence here from ancient Egyptian astronomy where four stars in the sky are connected to these exact points.

As far as their connection to embalming goes, it might be because they could help with mummification—or at least help protect against damage to corpses. Though there are many other roles that those four deities play, the closest thing to "encapsulation" (as with the four sons of Horus) is their general protecting role.

Chapter 40: Horus's Journey to the Underworld

Horus is the lord of the sky, and Re is the god of the sun, so Re's night seems to equate to Horus's journey through the underworld. When Re sets in his boat each evening, he descends beneath the western horizon; this marks Horus's entry into Duat, also known as "the house of Osiris" or "the hall of Osiris." Duat represents death for some Egyptians who believe that everyone has an immortal soul that lives after death. However, it is more likely thought of as a haven where one's shadow (khaibit) is sheltered from injury and harm. Hence, the ancient Egyptian alphabet represents the soul as a shadow called khaibit.

Horus' journey through Duat is also called his "journey of necessity" (di-um-ankh) in some inscriptions. Horus must travel into Duat with his eye upon Anubis to "give judgment" upon the dead. In this way, Horus is permitted to enter Duat himself. On his journey, Horus meets and speaks with various gods like Osiris and Isis, whom he battles against to gain back his eye (Orion's Eye), which had been stolen by Set during a dispute of their father Osiris' body with Seth. His journey is finally ended when he arrives at the gate of the gods where he meets Amun ("Horus, you have done well!" Amun says by way of greeting), and with a nod to Amun, Horus enters into the realm of Osiris.

The journey is also shown in more traditional representations. In one example, Set steals his brother's eye, and Horus rushes off to Duat to retrieve it. He summons Anubis to "give judgment" on the deceased. In this relief from Karnak, one sees Horus bring his eye back to restore order.

From this point on, Horus becomes a new sun god, just as Re was before him. Re had no son before becoming Osiris. Therefore, Horus is the son of Osiris, and Re's identity is a separate one. It explains why, in some myths, Horus and Set are enemies. It is also because they are brothers.

Horus's journey to the underworld is sometimes depicted by a young man with his left foot on the head of a jackal-headed god and holding a crook over his shoulder, and sometimes by a bearded adult with one foot on a jackal-headed god and holding a scepter over his shoulder. In other representations, he is shown as wearing the double crown of Egypt, one that looks like Re's crown and the other that looks like Osiris' crown.

Nut's Descent into the Underworld

As the worlds converged, the ancient Egyptian pantheon found itself in difficult times. Its existence became diminished as Ra, Thoth, Isis, and Osiris were no longer worshiped by people. To survive and live on, Nut became associated with the underworld between the end of the Old Kingdom and the beginning of the Middle Kingdom (approximately 2040 BC).

While it's generally agreed that Nut does not often appear in hieroglyphics or mythology before this time (i.e., after the Old Kingdom), it's also decided that some form of Nut was worshiped somewhere in Egypt for at least 9,000 years.

Therefore, the form of Nut during the Old Kingdom became widely recognized as the sky goddess Nut. Her name appears to have been a combination of the words *nwt* (which has no meaning) and *nut*. The word *nwt* is thought to have been allocated as a title used on one god or another. Hence, Nut also means "sky," and she is sometimes depicted as a cow because the Egyptians associated cattle with water and life.

It's believed that at some point before she became associated with death (i.e., after the Old Kingdom), she was related to the Milky Way. Her sister and husband were Geb and Osiris, respectively. It's often believed that

Nut became his wife when he became the ruler of the underworld instead of Seth; however, there is nothing to suggest this in Egyptian mythology or hieroglyphics. It's thought that Nut's sister-husband relationship with Osiris came about because of her later role as earth goddess (i.e., after the Old Kingdom).

Nut was worshipped primarily at Heliopolis and on papyrus scrolls, where she was often portrayed as a cow or as a naked woman with a star or horns upon her head between two mountains. As a goddess of the sky, it was believed that Nut gave birth to the sun every morning and swallowed it each evening.

Nut's other central role is a protector of deceased souls. She's often shown kneeling on the last body of Osiris and holding his hand while Nephthys is sitting over his shoulder. Sometimes she's sitting over Re to protect him too. However, this is not so common and therefore thought to be a later Egyptian tradition. In this capacity, Nut becomes associated with Isis and Hathor, as Isis protects Osiris in life (i.e., Osiris was killed by his arch-enemy Seth) and Hathor saves Re in death (i.e., Re was killed by Set of the Ennead).

In most legends, it's written that Nut became the mother of the god Horus before she became associated with the underworld.

Chapter 41: The End and the Beginning

Egyptian mythology is rich with evolution, death, resurrection, life, and love. It is one of the oldest mythologies ever recorded in history, dating back to 3200 BC. The most well-known deity is Osiris, god of death. He was killed by his brother Set and then resurrected by Isis to be king of both earth and underworld (the dead). In ancient Egypt, death is not a tragic event but an honor. The idea that death progresses into a place of peace, comfort, and safety began as a concept in the Middle Ages, but the Egyptians certainly believed in it.

The gods do not live forever, and when they die, they leave behind their physical remains so that they may be worshipped in the afterlife. Many gods are dead and no longer honored. To be cherished, these gods have to be made tangible by being prepared for burial or cremation. Once this happens, their remains are either buried underground or burned as an offering to the gods. Although the idea of death is a little more clear-cut than that of life in Egyptian mythology, it is by far more complex. It is because life and death occur in cycles and are incredibly intertwined with each other. It is not always possible to define one event as the beginning and the other event as the end.

The Osiris myth begins with his death at the hands of Set. Osiris' wife, Isis, in her grief, decides to search for him after she hears from a cow herder (Amset) that Set killed him and threw him into a river. Isis suspects that Set buried her husband's body across the river. She searches for his body. This part of the myth is vital because Isis is looking for her husband because she feels guilty about his death so much. She wants to take care of him when she finds him even though they are no longer married. When found, she carries Osiris to an unfinished pyramid built by her father. She nurses him back to health to make up for killing him in the first place, but he eventually dies.

At this point, the gods intervene by sending a loyal servant of Osiris' named Anubis to Isis to cut off her embalming cloth so that Osiris can be reborn and make a new beginning without the pain of death. Once Anubis cuts off the fabric, Isis is forcibly removed from Osiris' body by Horus, who wants to take over as ruler of Egypt.

After Isis is removed from Osiris' body, he is placed in the tomb, and lionesses are placed around it for protection. He is buried alive with his sister Nephthys.

He is offered nourishment through his grave as a way of showing their love for him.

The end does not come without struggle. After being placed in the tomb, it is believed Osiris did not die right away, nor did he experience a peaceful rest. He was trapped in the darkness of the underworld and tortured by his brother Set, who beat him and threw him about until his death.

The curse of death is known as Heru and can be broken by Isis, who appears to several gods and goddesses to ask for their help in breaking this curse. At this point, Isis takes over her husband's body again, and she uses her magic to return Osiris to life. She resurrects him on a slab of rock, and he is welcomed back to life.

In Egyptian mythology, love and devotion to one's spouse will save people from death. Death may come eventually, but it can be avoided. A person can live a happy life with their loved ones who have passed away. The cycle of life and death appears to repeat itself. People die, but they are remembered forever by those who love them. In the myth, Isis and Osiris are married, and she is devoted to him despite her committing the crime of killing him in the first place. They have an ideal relationship as it shows what love can do.

The most important concept in Egyptian mythology is death and resurrection. Without it, we would not have the idea of spirituality or deities, such as Seth or Osiris, who were brought back to life after their death. One of the oldest myths ever written down has inspired many other cultures with its complexity, but it has a simple representation of the life-and-death cycle. The most famous resurrection story is the story of Osiris and Isis.

Egyptian mythology began from an ancient religion. The Egyptian religion came from their belief in an afterlife to which they would go after death. They often used other myths for their beliefs, including the Greek myth about Perseus and Andromeda. In the Greek myth, Perseus slays a sea monster and rescues Andromeda from the sea god, who took her as his bride. The only difference between it and the Egyptian myth is that Perseus actually marries Andromeda instead of Perseus going away. Egyptian myths deal with everyday life on earth, but they also include death because they believe that their religion is deeper than simple life on earth; they believe in an afterlife, where people will go after death.

Conclusion

One might argue that mythology is meant for adults and not teens, but with the explosion of Harry Potter and Percy Jackson books, it is no longer an argument. The world of Greek mythology, Norse mythology, and Egyptian mythology is fascinating, filled with epic stories of heroes and gods. These stories are just as valuable to us today as they were to ancient Greeks, Norse, and Egypt, who put them together. Now we have this opportunity to learn about these old tales in a modern way by taking on the young heroes who recreate them.

Although the names of many of the characters are still debated, there is a great deal that remains to be learned about these immortal figures. In this book, readers have learned about the Greek, Norse, and Egyptian gods and heroes, and they have seen how their stories remain relevant today.

Readers have learned about the Greek, Norse, and Egyptian gods and heroes, including who they are, where they came from, what their powers are, and what they looked like.

In addition to these myths being educational for teens in modern society, they are also entertaining. Myths give a better understanding of how life was back then. Readers have also found out that not all myths are true or accurate.

Finally, readers have learned about how the Greeks, Norsemen, and Egyptians view love and social interactions, as well as how they view death and the afterlife. These myths are not evil, and in some cases, they help us.

All in all, this book is an excellent introduction to Greek, Norse, and Egyptian mythology for teens. Unlike many different books on the topic, it approaches the matter with a positive attitude while still being informative and entertaining at the same time. Although most teens are familiar with these myths already due to their prominent role in popular culture, they still need to be updated on what their parents might have forgotten or missed when they were younger.

If you plan to teach yourself Greek, Norse, and Egyptian mythology, your first step should be to look for a dictionary or thesaurus. This book teaches you some of the most important terms and definitions in mythology to help you understand the myths.

Reading this book gives you an idea of Greek, Norse, and Egyptian mythology. It is for people who have a serious interest in mythology. If you'd like to get a brief overview of each of the different mythologies, this book is perfect for you.

Anyone who uses this guide gets the full spectrum of the stories, but it doesn't go into much detail—just enough to give readers a general idea of each thing. These myths are not taken too seriously by their faithful followers. They are enjoyable to read and not like a dull and plain history lesson.

Printed in Great Britain
by Amazon